DEATH IN
CENTRAL PARK

MARCY MICHAEL PUBLISHING
MARCYMICHAEL.COM

HARPER STANWICK, SR.

CONTENTS

CHAPTER ONE

"Is that your final decision?" Steve Collins asked, his voice taut with controlled urgency.

Stephanie Orton's eyes were fixed on her russet shoes, peeking and slipping away beneath the hem of her gown. Her silence lingered, resisting the pressure of the question. Finally, she lifted her gaze to meet Steve's, her brown eyes touched by a faint, reluctant smile that softened his stern expression.

"Yes, that is my final decision," she repeated, with deliberate slowness. Steve sank heavily onto a bench, his eyes drifting over the manicured lawn. His thoughts churned with a sense of unfairness he couldn't quite place. His devotion seemed unwarranted by the situation – loyal only to this unassuming girl who refused his proposal, simply because he had never dirtied his hands with labor or engaged his mind in anything more strenuous than idle distractions since his school days.

Steve was an unfortunate soul endowed with a spirit of laziness and a modest inheritance that, although it didn't make him rich, was ample enough to sustain his leisure. He lacked the driving necessity that pushed others to achieve. In essence, Steve was a fixture of society, contributing little, harming little. While many might call him ornamental, no one could deny his appeal, least of all Stephanie, whose expressive eyes traced his features with an unmistakable affection.

Taking off his straw hat, Steve absently ran his fingers through his tousled light hair, then crossed one leg over the other. His mind swirled in discontent. The frank, boyish look that had charmed so many was replaced by a dark, brooding frown, his bright blue eyes staring unseeingly at the picturesque landscape sprawling before him.

He couldn't fathom why a girl like Stephanie would entertain such wild ideas. Plenty of other women openly admired him, and he knew they were his for the asking. But for some reason, Stephanie captivated him more than anyone else. Her stubbornness and independence only made her more appealing, albeit frustratingly so.

Stephanie Orton was not a conventional beauty like Steve Collins. She was tall and slender, almost to the point of being bony, yet her grace and fluidity overshadowed her imperfections. Her murky complexion seemed to vanish when you gazed into her bright, expressive eyes, accentuated by a charming smile. Moreover, Stephanie was an heiress to a fortune exceeding a million dollars, which kept people from calling her plain. Orphaned at a young age, she had been raised by a practical old aunt who would likely leave her another hefty inheritance.

Stephanie was acutely aware of her imperfections, possibly even more so than others. She lacked vanity and possessed an uncommon amount of practical wisdom. She knew she wouldn't have to struggle to find a husband, yet her heart had been set on the dashing Steve Collins since the year before she graduated from Vassar. He had originally gone there to pursue another girl but ended up falling head over heels for Stephanie instead. Regardless, she was in no rush to get married. She loved Steve deeply, but there was an obstacle between them that only he could overcome.

"You know, Steve," she said softly, as he stared across the verdant lawn, struggling to make sense of his thoughts, "I've told you this before."

"Yes, this makes the sixth time I've proposed," he replied bitterly, still looking away.

"I've always told you," she continued, her smile faint and her voice lowered as she glanced warily at a girl seated nearby, "I won't marry you as long as you live the way you do."

I have enough money for both of us, so it doesn't matter if the man I marry has any or not. But I can't and won't marry someone worthless—someone who's never done anything and is too lazy to start. I want a husband with some abilities, someone who's achieved at least one meaningful thing. After that, well, it wouldn't matter so much if he became lazy. You know, Steve, how much I care for you," she said softly, "how fond I am of you, but I won't marry you until you prove you can accomplish something."

"It's easy for you to say," he replied bitterly, "but what can I do? I can't risk what little I have on Wall Street. I don't know enough to be a preacher, a doctor, or a lawyer, and it's too damned long to start from scratch. You don't want me following the races, and I couldn't sell ribbons or run a hotel to save my life. Tell me what to do, Stephanie, and I'll try it. When you got that idea to walk in the park at a ridiculous hour every morning, before your friends, who think it's bad form, could see and judge, didn't I promise to be your escort? And haven't I kept that promise, whether I had to get up early or stay up all night?"

"And how many times have you been late?" she asked playfully.

"Stephanie, don't," he pleaded. "You know I love you. If I thought your stubbornness would keep us apart forever, I'd— Oh, darling, please don't doubt my love."

"Hush!" she whispered, warningly, pointing to the girl on the other bench.

"Oh, she's asleep," Steve replied nonchalantly.

"Don't be too sure," Stephanie urged, gazing thoughtfully at the girl, her eyes softened by the feelings that surged in her heart.

Like most women, Stephanie never grew tired of hearing the man she loved profess his devotion. But, as with many, she preferred to be the only one listening to those heartfelt vows.

"If she's awake, she's the first girl I've ever seen who'd let her new La Tosca sunshade lie on the ground," he laughed.

"She must be asleep," Stephanie replied nonchalantly, glancing at the parasol lying in the dust, as if it had slipped from the girl's knee. Two gray squirrels, with their bushy tails poised upright, scampered onto the dusty path. Seeing everything quiet, they dashed across to the lush grass, standing upright to curiously observe the uneasy lovers. Stephanie had a habit of carrying peanuts to the park for the animals. She pulled several from her purse and tossed them toward the squirrels. One let out a little whistle before scurrying up the nearest tree, while the other grabbed a nut in its mouth and quickly followed.

"I haven't seen her move since we got here," Stephanie commented, returning to the subject of the girl. "Do you think she pulled her hat over her eyes to block out the light, or maybe she's trying to avoid being seen?"

"I'm not sure," he said, dismissively. "Maybe she's not feeling well."

"Not well? You really think so, Steve? I'm going to check on her," Stephanie declared impulsively.

"Don't," Steve urged. "I wouldn't."

"But I will," Stephanie insisted.

"You don't know anything about her," he continued, trying to dissuade her. "She might have been out all night, or who knows, maybe she's had too much to drink. If you wake her, she could cause a scene."

"How uncharitable of you," Stephanie said indignantly. She feared no one. Having spent much of her time and money on charitable deeds, she had encountered all kinds of women. The mere fact that a woman might be in trouble and that she could help was enough for Stephanie.

She stood and walked over to the girl. Steve, aware that any protest would be futile, followed her. When they stopped, Stephanie leaned down and peeked beneath the brim of the lace hat, heavily adorned with red roses, which was tilted over the motionless girl's face.

"She's asleep," she whispered softly to Steve. "Her eyes are closed. She has a beautiful face."

"Does she now?" Steve, with renewed curiosity, bent down to take a look. "She's incredibly pale. I'm afraid she might be sick," he murmured, a note of awe in his voice. "Miss?" he called nervously. The girl didn't move. Steve and Stephanie exchanged a glance, a swift shared look of surprise and fear.

"My dear!" Stephanie said, gently shaking the girl by the shoulder. The lace hat slipped off and fell at their feet; the girl's hands, which had been loosely folded in her lap, fell apart, and her body slowly slumped sideways on the bench. Breathless and silent, the young couple stared at the beautiful upturned face framed by golden hair; the blue-rimmed eyes, their dark lashes resting against pale skin; the parted lips that retained a hint of red. Nervously, Steve touched her cheek, then felt for a heartbeat and a pulse.

"What's the matter there?" A gray-uniformed officer called out, leaving his horse at the edge of the walkway. Stephanie looked to Steve, waiting for him to respond. As he raised his face, white with horror, he gasped:

"My God! The girl's dead."

CHAPTER TWO

Steve Collins wasn't wrong. The golden-haired girl was dead. Her fair figure was taken to the morgue, and for several days, the newspapers were abuzz with the Central Park mystery. Everyone was talking about it, and who wouldn't be captivated by such an enigma? A young, stunningly beautiful girl, dressed in stylish yet understated clothing typically worn by women of refinement, found lifeless on a bench in Central Park by two young people from high society, where any brush with scandal is almost a disgrace.

What heightened the mystery was that an exhaustive examination of her body revealed no wounds, discoloration, or even a hint of the cause of death. The newspapers spawned a multitude of theories. Some firmly believed it was a case of foul play, but they couldn't explain the method or how someone could murder such a lovely girl in Central Park without a trace and then escape unnoticed. Other papers scoffed at the idea of foul play, suggesting instead that she had either succumbed to heart disease or taken poison herself while sitting on the bench.

The police maintained a veil of impenetrable secrecy but promised startling developments in a few days. They were careful not to speculate publicly on how she had died. This silence was strategic; a quiet investigator is often assumed to know much more than one who spills details freely. Thus, the public waited impatiently, confident the police would soon unravel the mystery.

Hundreds of people crowded the morgue, all eager to glimpse the dead girl who had become the center of this captivating mystery.

Many people came looking for missing friends, hoping and fearing that they'd find their lost loved one in the mysterious dead girl. People from distant places telegraphed, asking for the body to be kept until they arrived, but they came and went, leaving the beautiful dead girl still unidentified. Stephanie Orton and Steve Collins were thrust into the spotlight in all the stories about the enigma, much to their discomfort. Persistent reporters showed up at Stephanie's door at all hours, each new theory giving them a reason to drag her name into the public eye again. Poor Steve found no peace at his club, his apartment, or even at Stephanie's place. If he wasn't being interviewed by the press, his friends bombarded him with questions about the strange case, constantly begging him to retell the story of the body's discovery. Some of his club acquaintances even made jokes about the girl he had found dead, and there was much quiet laughter among his close friends at Steve's newfound reputation for early morning walks, a habit highlighted by his involvement in this now- famous case.

A key figure in the drama was the Park policeman who found Stephanie and Steve bending over the dead girl. Overnight, he became quite the celebrity. His previous notable deeds involved finding a lost child and frantically chasing a stray dog, which he mistakenly thought was rabid, firing wildly at it until the scared animal vanished. This officer suddenly became the envy of all the Park policemen. Daily, his name was mentioned in connection with the case as "the brave officer of the 'Mystery of Central Park.'" People thronged to the spot where the girl had been found, curious to see the bench and to take away some small keepsake.

Officer Danvers always found himself near the mystery's epicenter during the Park's peak hours, handling the barrage of questions about specifics with a certain gravitas. It wasn't surprising he took pride in being linked to such a high-profile case. New York buzzed with unprecedented excitement over the enigma of the girl's death. Newspapers detailed every aspect of her elegant silk lingerie, her meticulously crafted Directoire dress, her suede shoes, the silver-handled La Tosca sunshade. They lingered over descriptions of her delicate hands and feet, her flawless features, and her abundant, radiant yellow hair. Everything about her spoke of sophistication and opulence. So how was it possible that someone so captivating and poised had nobody to miss her, nobody to scour the Earth seeking her whereabouts?

The day of the inquest arrived. Stephanie, along with her aunt and Steve, had no choice but to attend. With a remarkably steady voice, Stephanie recounted how they had discovered the body. She faced intense questioning about why she felt compelled to approach someone who appeared to be merely asleep. It was an unusual act. Didn't she think she might have been influenced by the young man accompanying her? Stephanie's indignation flared as they tried to insinuate a closer connection between Steve and the incident. She recalled everything that transpired with such precision that it later sparked whispers she had rehearsed her story to shield the real culprit.

Steve was next. His account mirrored Stephanie's, and though no one outright accused him of withholding the truth, the suspicions were palpable in every question, every scrutinizing glance. He could feel the weight of their doubts pressing upon him, an unspoken accusation that gnawed at his core.

A savvy newspaper had just that morning published an in-depth article, highlighting instances where murderers couldn't stay away from their victims and often returned to the scene, sometimes pretending to be the one who discovered the body. The article concluded by calling on the authorities to determine, at the inquest, who was responsible for the murder of the beautiful young girl. Remembering all this, Steve felt his heart pound with indignation at the tone of his examiner. Stephanie was even more incensed than Steve, but she had read a different article that dismissed the murder theory, listing deaths initially deemed suspicious but later proven to be due to heart disease or poisoning. She quietly hoped that the doctors conducting the post-mortem would dispel any doubts in this case.

The park policeman dramatically gave his testimony. He recounted how he found the young couple bent over the dead girl, who was slumped on a bench. When he asked what was wrong, the young man, who appeared both excited and frightened—he stressed these words—replied, "The girl is dead." The officer had then looked at the body without touching it. The young couple denied knowing the girl's identity, but the officer, his suspicions aroused, asked the young man why he said, "The girl is dead," if he didn't know her. The young man insisted he had never seen the dead girl before, and at that moment, his companion shot him a quick, frightened glance. The officer then sternly warned:

"Be careful, young man. Remember, you are talking to the law; I'll have to report everything you say."

The officer paused to catch his breath and to lend weight to his words. Everyone took this moment to shift their gaze from the officer to see how Steve Collins was holding up.

Intrigue tightened its grip on nearly everyone in the room as the elegant young man seemed destined for custody by the close of the inquest. The officer cleared his throat and, with a deep, authoritative voice, continued his recounting. When he issued his warning, the young man's face had turned a fiery red, then drained of color, before he brazenly called the officer a fool. Nevertheless, the diligent officer pressed further, intent on unraveling the strange behavior of these two young people: not only driving but also walking early in the park and stumbling upon the dead body of a young girl. He questioned why, if the young man didn't know the girl, he didn't say "a girl is dead here," but rather "the girl is dead." The young man retorted once more that the officer was a fool, embellishing his insult, while the young girl, having remained solemnly silent up to that point, had the audacity to laugh.

Steve Collins was called up again, reiterating his reason for the early morning walk in the park and detailing his activities the previous evening, corroborated by Stephanie and her aunt. The inquiry into his linguistic choices—using "the girl" instead of "a girl"—yielded no satisfactory explanation. The law found it highly suspicious that a man unfamiliar with the deceased would refer to her in such a specific manner and exhibit such overt distress over her death.

Despite stirring suspicions, only a few more testimonies of little consequence were heard before the doctors who conducted the post-mortem examination were summoned. Their findings, or rather the lack thereof, heightened the mystery. No evidence hinted at murder or suicide, and frustratingly, they couldn't determine a clear cause of death.

The coroner's jury delivered an ambiguous verdict, revealing they knew no more about the circumstances or cause of the girl's death than they had at the start of the inquest. With this unsatisfactory conclusion, the public had to be content. They did know that the girl hadn't been shot or stabbed, which was some solace, at least. Stephanie convinced her aunt and Steve to accompany her through the Morgue. She felt deeply hurt by how Steve had been treated but still wanted to see the face of the young girl, the source of all their distress, before she was laid to rest.

"How dreadful!" exclaimed Stephanie's aunt, as the keeper unlocked the door and waited for them to enter the low room before closing it. She tiptoed carefully over the wet stone floor, holding her skirts up with one hand and using a perfumed handkerchief to cover her aristocratic nose with the other. Stephanie, her face serious but calm, stayed close to the keeper, while Steve walked silently beside the aunt.

"I thought the bodies lay on marble slabs," said Stephanie, glancing at the row of plain, unpainted wooden boxes set close together on iron supports.

"They did in the old Morgue, but since we've moved to this building, we put them in these boxes. They keep better this way," the keeper explained, clearly delighted to show the Morgue to people of social standing.

"Do you know the history of all these dead?" asked Stephanie, counting the more than fifty coffins lined up one after the other.

"We know something about most of them, except those found in the river, and the river provides more bodies than the whole city does. We photograph every body and store their clothes with a description, keeping them for six months. We keep the photographs indefinitely, so that even years later, people might find their lost ones here."

"Would you like to see them, miss?"

The man's voice echoed in the dimly lit room as he lifted a heavy lid. "You see," he explained, "we mark a cross on the coffins of the

Catholics. The Protestants, they get no mark. The boxes with the chalk marks are set to be buried tomorrow. This man here," he gestured at another lid, "was a streetcar driver. Want to take a look, miss?"

Stephanie's aunt shook her head firmly.

"He went on strike and couldn't find work afterward. His family was starving, so he decided to make things easier by taking his own life."

"It's so hard to die," Stephanie said, her voice trembling.

"Hard? Not at all, miss. Death's a mercy for the poor. Now, this one here," he continued, lifting another lid. Stephanie stared into the lifeless eyes of a weather-beaten man, his face etched with countless premature wrinkles but surprisingly peaceful. "They think he was a tramp. Collapsed on Sixth Avenue with nothing on him to identify who he was. And this woman," he pointed to another coffin nearby. "She's lying next to the 'Park Mystery Girl.' She smiles as if she got something she wanted. They almost all smile when they've settled their accounts. This one," he said, gesturing to the woman, "was infamous. She did time on the island and was in and out of Blackwell's Insane Asylum, but it was no good. As soon as she got out, she went back to her old ways. Drink, fight, steal—anything to get her fix. They picked her up on the sidewalk and brought her to the station-house. By morning, she was gone. When they checked her, they assumed she was just drunk, but they found out she had taken her final trip to an island where there's no return."

Just then, a small, plump woman in a shabby black dress and plain black bonnet entered, escorted by one of the keeper's assistants.

She clutched a rough white cotton handkerchief in her hand, her wrinkled, broad face—fish-like mouth, thick, upturned nose, and watery blue eyes—ready to show grief once their search among the labeled rough-boxes bore fruit.

"Mrs. Lang, from the Almshouse?" read the man helping her search.

"Yes, that's her name. God rest her soul," she replied fervently. The man slid the lid across the box, and the little old woman, handkerchief pressed to her nose, peered inside.

"Yes, that's her; that's Mrs. Lang. Poor thing! Oh, she looks so lonely," she lamented. "She didn't have a single friend in the world," she continued, her weak eyes meeting Stephanie's compassionate gaze. Stephanie had paused nearby, touched by the scene. "She was eighty years old and paralyzed from the knees down. They took her to the Almshouse not even a month ago, and now look at her. Poor Mrs. Lang, she looks so desolate."

The man, feeling she'd had enough time to mourn, closed the box, and the wailing woman exited.

"What happens to the bodies of these poor souls?" Stephanie asked, her voice catching.

"Most of them go to medical colleges for study. Men and women, black and white alike. That woman over there, the one who wouldn't betray her assailant, is going to a college tonight. The bodies that aren't sold are sent to Hart Island, where they're buried in a big trench."

Stephanie's empathetic nature quivered with pity at what she'd witnessed and heard.

Stephanie quietly decided to give the unidentified girl a proper burial. She planned to add some flowers to the makeshift coffins that would be taken to the Potter's Field tomorrow.

"Death is such a dreadful thing," she said sadly as they re-entered through the iron doors.

"It surely is, miss," the keeper agreed. "I've been in charge of this Morgue for twenty years now, but if I let myself ponder too much about death and what lies beyond, I'd lose my mind."

"But thinking about Heaven might offer some comfort," Stephanie said hesitantly.

"Twenty years in there," he said, nodding his head toward the eerie chamber where death always reigns, where the only sound is the constant dripping of water. "It's enough to strip any illusions about the afterlife. We live, and when we die, that's the end of it. You can tell kids about the 'good man' and 'bad man,' Heaven and Hell—just like you tell them about Santa Claus—but when they grow up, if they think for themselves, they'll realize it's all fairy tales. When you're dead, you're dead, and that's it. Trust me on that."

Stephanie wasn't overly religious, but his blunt words jarred her few spiritual beliefs. She pulled her shoulders back, her warm expression chilled, making her seem less approachable. She felt a slight wave of repulsion toward the disbelieving Morgue keeper. It wasn't that his views were entirely foreign to thoughts she had herself; she often had her own doubts. Yet, she felt it was her duty to suppress those doubts and hold onto the teachings about the afterlife that she'd grown up with.

Stephanie rejoined her aunt and Steve Collins, who were waiting for her under the shade tree across from the Morgue. She quickly explained her plan. Her kind- hearted aunt smiled encouragingly at her.

Maybe what they had witnessed left its mark on her too. Instead of heading straight to her place, they went to the coroner's office. With the permit quickly secured, they moved on to an undertaker's to arrange the girl's burial. So, the enigmatic beauty from Central Park wasn't destined for a medical college or Potter's Field.

The next morning, Stephanie joined Steve in his coupe, while her aunt, Mrs. Louise Van Brunt, followed in her carriage, accompanied by two elderly, charitable friends. They trailed the somber hearse as it slowly crossed the bridge to Brooklyn. In a serene cemetery on the city's outskirts, they laid the girl to rest. Throughout the journey, Stephanie remained deeply troubled. She sat quietly, her mind in turmoil. Steve, sensing her mood, also stayed silent and pensive.

The case had deeply unsettled Stephanie. It wasn't just about the unknown girl; the underlying suspicions about Steve gnawed at her. Though she never doubted his innocence, dark thoughts about his past—whispered rumors of affairs with actresses, hinted at by the newspapers—tormented her. Could it be that he knew the girl, or had seen her before they found her lifeless? She recalled his shock when he first saw her face on that park bench. The officer had emphasized Steve's apparent agitation, and now, looking back, it seemed to imply more than what he had admitted.

"And I love him, I love him," she silently despaired during the long ride to the cemetery. "But with this dreadful suspicion hanging over him, I could never marry him; I could never be happy if I did. And yet, I can never be happy if I don't."

"If only we knew more about it; if people didn't just drop hints; if I could shake off this terrible idea that he knows more than he's letting on!"

They got out of the carriage and moved quietly through the cemetery, weaving between the grassy and flower-filled graves marked by white stones that once symbolized life and hope. An unknown minister, Christian by his attire, stood ready by the open grave. Stephanie glanced at him, then at the workers who had been lounging under a nearby tree. As they saw the group approaching, the workers came over with expressions that held only idle curiosity. The minister murmured the burial service softly while the coffin was lowered into the ground. Stephanie's throat felt tight, her heart pounded painfully as Steve, his expression somber, dropped some flowers into the grave.

"Oh death, how awful, how terrible!" she thought. "And I, too, will die someday; be laid in a grave, and then what? What did we do to our Creator to deserve death? This poor girl! This is her end for all eternity, and no one she knew is here to witness it, unless..." But the dark suspicion about Steve refused to take clearer shape. The grave diggers were the most carefree among them. They removed a board, sending the pile of fresh earth beside the grave crashing down onto the coffin and the flowers, almost cheerfully, it seemed to Stephanie. She shivered slightly but watched, transfixed, until the men placed the last shovelful and deftly shaped the mound with their spades. Steve helped her cover the freshly made grave with the flowers and green ivy they had brought. They were the last to leave. The others had wandered among the graves and back to where the carriages waited.

As the hearse sped away, almost eager to collect its next passenger, the workmen with their shovels and picks vanished, leaving behind a fresh grave.

"It's over," Steve said with a sigh of relief as he escorted Stephanie back to her car. "Now, let's put these painful days behind us and find some happiness."

"It's not over," Stephanie retorted, her voice firm and determined. "It's just beginning. I can't be happy until I uncover the true cause of that girl's death."

"That's impossible, Stephanie," Steve replied. "It's a mystery that will never be solved."

"Steve," she said, breathlessly, "you've promised you love me, and you've vowed to do anything I ask if I agree to marry you. Did you mean it? Will you promise me again?"

"Mean it, my love?" Steve echoed, pressing her hand tightly against his heart. "I swear it on my life."

"Then uncover the mystery of that girl's death," Stephanie demanded, "and I will be your wife."

CHAPTER THREE

S teve Collins Was In Despair. Days Had Slipped By Since They Buried The Unknown Girl, And He Was No Closer To Solving The Mystery Than The Morning They Found Her. He Hadn't Uncovered A Single New Clue, And What Was Even Worse, He Had No Idea Where To Start. He Aimlessly Roamed The City's Streets, Tormented By A Growing Sense Of Hopelessness.

"Good Lord, if only I had a lead," he muttered to himself as he wandered down Fifth Avenue. "If I only knew where to begin, what to look for, or even just the first step. Damn it, why did she have to die right in front of us? Why couldn't someone else have found her instead? As if I didn't have enough to deal with already. Why must women be so maddeningly unpredictable? If I wasn't suspected of being involved in her death, and if Stephanie... But damn it, I can't just ignore this. It's either solve the mystery or lose Stephanie! If I only knew how to make a start. But, honestly, I could preach a sermon, set a broken leg, or even cook a dinner more easily than figure out how, when, or why that blonde girl died. Curse my luck."

"I've read plenty of stories where some clueless guy ends up solving a murder, but they always stumble upon evidence that all the detectives and police missed, giving them the perfect clue to work on. It makes for great fiction, but here, there's nothing. The others are just as sharp, maybe even sharper at finding clues, and they've got nothing. I've got nothing. Figuring this out would baffle Solomon himself."

Steve's restless steps had brought him to Stephanie's home. He stopped and looked up at her windows, feeling the weight of the unsolved mystery and the pressing need to clear his name.

He hadn't seen her for two days; buried in his case, he sent her a groaning email, followed by a bouquet of roses, and then set off to waste another day in aimless wandering. But here, standing before her door, how could a lover resist the temptation to step inside and bask in her presence for even a few moments? Steve was never one for resistance, so after a brief hesitation, he bounded up the broad stone steps and was welcomed into Stephanie's sanctuary. Her room, part library, part study, was nothing short of enchanting.

The space radiated luxury and taste, a haven for a young woman with an eye for beauty. Heavy drapes hung around, a plush carpet covered the floor, accentuated by fine rugs thrown leisurely over low divans. Chairs and lounges in various cozy shapes invited relaxation. Little tables held a treasure trove of rich bric-a-brac. Unique spirit lamps cast a warm glow, while paintings and etchings, each with its own tale, adorned the walls. Fine statues – some sculpted by Stephanie herself – added to the room's allure.

A low organ stood beside a piano light, open and ready, with music sheets and books scattered in abundance. Near where the daylight was strongest sat a flat- top desk, cluttered with papers, cards, and the myriad inconsequential trinkets that a refined woman instinctively gathers. The most unusual sight – bound to catch the eye of any rare visitor – was a mixed collection of odd canes and weapons. In the center of the desk, a skull had been ingeniously repurposed as an inkstand and penholder.

"Well, Steve," Stephanie said as she glided in, wearing an elegant gray carriage gown. "I'm glad to see you."

"I wish you'd arrived earlier; we could have enjoyed a drive with Aunt and me," Stephanie said.

"I've been busy," Steve admitted, letting go of the hand she had offered upon their greeting. They settled on the sofa together.

"I've been so tied up that I haven't had time for a drive these last few days."

"Have you discovered anything yet?" Stephanie asked eagerly, her eyes bright with curiosity.

"Well, not exactly," Steve responded hesitantly. "It'll take some time to unravel everything, you know."

"Tell me, do you know her name yet? Where she came from? Was she really murdered?"

"Easy now; would you have me ruin my chances by revealing everything I've found?" Steve replied evasively, a mischievous sparkle in his eyes.

"Oh, you superstitious boy," laughed Stephanie, playfully tapping his hand. He grasped her hand, keeping it firmly in his own.

"Don't be unkind," he pleaded as she tried to pull her hand away.

"Not for the world," she replied solemnly, stopping her resistance. "Mr. John Stetson Maxwell visited last night. He shared an experience from when he was an editor, which made me resolve never to speak or act unkindly if I can help it."

"I owe Mr. Maxwell a great debt," Steve quipped.

"But it was very sad, Steve. It weighed on me all evening."

"I wish my own miseries could have the same effect on you," he said with a laugh.

"Don't you want to hear the story? I meant to tell you," she said, a hint of irritation in her voice over his flippancy.

"Of course. Please, go on," he replied, immediately serious. He never joked when she adopted that tone and look.

"When he was an editor," she began softly, "he once received a brilliant poem from a man in Buffalo. He didn't know the man as a writer, but the poem was so exceptional that he accepted it right away and sent a note along with a check for the work. A few days later, the man's card was sent in, requesting an interview. Mr...."

Maxwell was swamped with work, but he decided to spare a moment for the visitor, so he asked the boy to bring him up. When the visitor arrived, Maxwell was taken aback to see a young man, probably around twenty-five. The young man's clothes were shabby, and he seemed visibly nervous in front of someone as influential as Editor Maxwell.

"Yes, yes," Steve said kindly, patting her hands reassuringly.

"Mr. Maxwell later remembered that the young man looked utterly dejected," Stephanie continued with a measured smile. "At the time, he was too pressed for time to notice much, and editors are accustomed to encountering people down on their luck. Maxwell brusquely inquired about the young man's business, noticing he was hesitant to speak. The young man simply mentioned he had come to the city and was curious to see the office. Maxwell summoned a boy to give the young man a tour and dismissed him soon after. A few days later, Maxwell received a batch of poetry from the same young man. Although the poems were remarkably good, Maxwell found them too melancholic for his publication and sent them back with a standard rejection slip.

Shortly thereafter, Maxwell was horrified to read about the young man's death. The young man had gone to the park, sat on a bench by the lake, and shot himself. His body wasn't discovered until the next day. In his pocket was a letter requesting that his body be cremated. He had enough money for the cremation expenses and left instructions that one of his friends could do as they wished with his ashes."

"Well, many people do the same thing," Steve said, somewhat insensitively.

"Yes, but this case was especially tragic," Stephanie insisted. "The young man was completely alone. He didn't have a single relative in the world."

He had clawed his way up from nothing and just finished law school, but hadn't yet landed any clients. He was struggling, and Mr. Maxwell believes, as do I, that he felt so uplifted when one of his poems was accepted that he traveled to the city, hoping to ask the editor for a job. But when he was greeted with such cold indifference, he lost the courage to explain why he had come. Back in Buffalo, as a final grasp at hope, he penned more poems filled with his own melancholy. When they were all rejected, it broke him. He went out and took his own life.

"But what else could Mr. Maxwell have done, Stephanie?" Steve asked pragmatically. "He couldn't publish work that wasn't fit for his magazine. How could he blame himself for that?"

"I can, and so can he," she replied firmly. "It would have taken no more time to be kind to that man than it did to be cruel. Instead of sending back that harsh, pre-printed rejection, he could have had his assistant write a simple note, saying the poems, though good, weren't right for his publication. It would have softened the blow, at least."

"But editors don't have time for that, Stephanie."

"Then they should make time."

"I swear it takes less time to be kind than unkind," Stephanie insisted, nodding adamantly.

"If bore's speeches weren't brief, they'd consume all their time," Steve shot back.

"Enough, Steve," she said with a dismissive wave, adopting that authoritative tone women use when they feel a losing argument. "There's no excuse for a man's brutality or unkindness."

Steve held his own views but wisely chose not to press Stephanie to share them.

"I'm leaving," she announced, seizing the chance to change the subject. "My aunt was invited to Washington to visit Mrs. Senator, and I'm going with her. I dread the trip, but Auntie thinks people there won't be as nosy about the Park mystery. I won't have to deal with reporters."

"I hope you're right," Steve replied, already feeling the hollow emptiness that gripped him whenever Stephanie left the city. As long as she was in town, even if they didn't see each other, he felt a sense of contentment knowing she was near. But her absence left him feeling as desolate as Adam must have felt before Eve.

"Stephanie," he began, a sudden idea sparking hope, "could we get engaged while I work on this case? We wouldn't have to tell anyone but your aunt, and it would mean so much to me. It would be a source of encouragement and happiness. You see, solving this mystery might take months." Steve feared it would take years. "But with your promise, I could conquer anything. It would give me the strength to take on the world."

"Don't be heartless, dear; don't be cruel to the one who loves you more than anything on this earth or beyond."

"Not now, Steve, you need to wait," replied Stephanie. "Wait until we solve the mystery. It shouldn't take too long" (Steve sighed) "and then, and then..."

"And then?" Steve echoed, his voice laced with hope. She glanced down, her cheeks flushing. He encircled her slender waist, drawing her close. "Then, my love? My soul?"

"Dearest, come here!" called Stephanie's aunt in that impeccably polite voice of hers that charmed all listeners but currently grated on Steve's nerves. "Steve, come, I need you to see the man standing across the Avenue. I've been watching him, and I think he's watching the house. Are we ever going to be done with this Park mystery business?"

They all peered cautiously through the curtains and unanimously agreed—the man was definitely watching the house for some reason.

"They're after you, Steve," exclaimed Stephanie. "Oh, I'm so afraid this will bring serious trouble your way."

Steve thought so too, but only where Stephanie was concerned; he kept his fears to himself.

"My dear child," laughed the aunt with that soothing tone. "Don't talk such nonsense! Steve can handle himself, especially now that he knows someone is following him."

Shortly afterward, Steve bid Stephanie farewell. She tried to put on a cheerful front, but her sad eyes betrayed her, hinting at the tears just beneath the surface. Grabbing his walking stick, Steve quickly left the house. His mood was so grim he felt almost vicious. He thought about the man watching the house and was half-tempted to hunt him down and confront him.

Sure enough, the man was there. As Steve started down the avenue, the man followed on the opposite side, like a disobedient dog that had been told to stay home. Steve flagged down a passing cab after walking a short distance, and almost immediately, the man got into another one. Steve wasn't up for being tailed, so he jumped out when he spotted an empty taxi, and, hiring it, told the driver to head across town. He didn't travel far, just enough to ensure he had shaken off his pursuer. Not feeling hungry yet, he told the driver to take him to Central Park, where he paid and dismissed him. Alone now, Steve felt a strong urge to visit the scene of the mystery that threatened his peace of mind.

"I'll go there and think it over," he thought. "Maybe it'll give me some ideas on how to unravel this." He retraced the path he and Stephanie had taken that dreadful morning. Night was closing in, and the Park was deserted except for the occasional workman hurrying home. The stillness was overwhelming, and his thoughts turned to the officer who had been such a nuisance. He wondered if policemen were on duty in the Park at night. He couldn't recall ever seeing any during his few evening visits, and there were none in sight now. He paused briefly at the bench where they had found the girl, before continuing to a bench near the reservoir. Sitting down and lighting a cigarette, he surrendered to his sorrowful thoughts about his predicament.

"If only fate would throw me a bone to help solve this mystery," he mused. "Unless something extraordinary happens, I'll never figure it out."

Stephanie is convinced it was murder, but I can't see what evidence she has for it. She believes it was a carefully planned crime, simply because nobody has come forward to claim the girl. Sometimes, I think she might be right, but proving it—that's the tricky part.

Steve gazed intently at the patch of light formed by the reservoir's opening, leading into the dense grove where night seemed perched, waiting to descend on any stragglers. As he stared, he noticed something moving between him and the light. Though a brave young man, his pulse quickened as he strained his eyes to identify the object. It moved again—this time, he could make out a shape climbing. In a moment, it was on the reservoir's edge. Outlined starkly against the sliver of the lit sky, he saw the figure of a woman, a slender girl with flowing hair.

In a flash, a dreadful thought pierced his mind—had she come here to end her life? Was she planning to commit suicide? With a choked cry of horror, he sprinted toward her.

Chapter Four

S teve Collins Sat Pensively On A Bench, Half Supporting The Frail Form Of The Girl He Had Just Saved From Death. He Had Caught Her Just As She Threw Up Her Hands With A Pitiful, Weak Cry, Poised To Leap Into The Reservoir.

"My dear young woman, don't be so downcast," he said, exasperatedly, as the girl leaned against his shoulder, sobbing in a heartbroken, distracted manner. "You're safe now."

As if that could console someone who had sought death and found none.

"Honestly, I'm sorry, but come on, don't cry," he said, trying to comfort her awkwardly. "I acted on impulse; if I'd known how upset you'd be, I swear, upon my honor, I wouldn't have intervened. I haven't got much to live for either, but seeing you so desperate was shocking. Now that it's all over, don't cry anymore. I'd laugh it off if I were you, like it was some kind of joke. Maybe the fates have something special planned for you. Look, that's better. You're not hurt—not even wet."

The girl broke into a nervous, hysterical laugh, her sobs still battling for dominance. Steve, much relieved, added a laugh that sounded rather hollow.

"I c-can't help it," she said haltingly, trying to stop her sobs. "It feels so unreal to still be living when I wanted to be dead. I-I thought it all through, and it was comforting, thinking it would all be over. No more seeing, thinking, hearing, or suffering. Oh, why did you stop me?"

"I didn't understand, you see. I thought you might regret it, that you were making a mistake," he said, trying to sound cheerful.

"What right does anyone—what right did you have to stop me from ending my life? I don't want to live! I'm tired of life and of misery."

"What right does anyone have to force me into a life that only brings me misery?" Kelly shouted, her voice quivering with indignation.

"Hey, don't get so downhearted." In the face of her anger, Steve regained his composure. "Tell me what's going on; maybe I can help. What's gone wrong?"

"Has anything ever gone right? Spare me your lectures. It's easy to sit there and preach when you've got friends, money, and a home. Save it for someone else. I've got nothing! I'm all alone in this big, heartless world. Not a cent to my name, no home, no friends. I'm just tired of it all. No point in talking. Some people get everything, and others get nothing. I'm one of the unlucky ones and the only thing left for me is to die."

"Come on now, there's got to be something better than death."

"Better? It's all just trouble and hunger, with occasional work. Do you call that better than death?" she cried, her desperation palpable. Her few words painted a grim picture. But Steve, carefree and fortunate, couldn't fully grasp their depth. He only saw that Kelly was deeply depressed, and thought it might do her good to talk about her troubles. How our problems can seem insurmountable when we keep them inside, and how small they become when shared with someone else. Steve spoke to her with his usual straightforward and optimistic manner, and before long, Kelly began to unburden herself, sharing the simple, poignant tale of her life.

Her name was Kelly Morgan. She'd grown up in the countryside, the only child of a village doctor. Her father had provided a comfortable life, but died with nothing left. Her mother had passed away at her birth. Raised well, Kelly's pride wouldn't allow her to take on menial work in her village. So after her father's death, she made her way to New York.

She quickly discovered that without experience or references, landing a decent job in New York was near impossible. When all else failed, she desperately sought and secured a position at a paper-box factory. Luckily, she picked up the skills fast and within a few months, earned as much as the best workers. She rented a small room on the top floor of a large tenement, where she slept and cooked her meals. Despite her paltry wages, she managed to save a little each week. One day, a girl who worked at the same table and had long been her friend, fainted. The other girls gathered around as she knelt on the floor, trying to revive her friend by bathing her head and rubbing her hands.

"Aha! Away from your tables during work hours. I'll make you pay for this, I'll dock each one of you," the foreman bellowed as he stormed into the workroom. Frightened, the girls quietly returned to their tasks, but she continued to tend to the fainted girl.

"You, down there, ignoring me, eh? I'll dock you twice," the foreman snarled as he noticed her behind the table. She looked up at him with such contempt that, if looks could kill, he would have dropped dead. Still, she managed to respond calmly.

"Maggie Williams fainted."

"And because one girl faints, the whole shop should stop working and break the rules? I'll make you all pay for this. I'll teach you," he vowed as he left the room. Undeterred by his threats, she continued to focus on Maggie, who soon opened her eyes and tried to get up.

"Stay still for a bit, Maggie," she urged. "Rest your head on my knee. Feeling better now?"

But Maggie didn't reply.

Her small gray eyes stared unblinkingly at the smoke-stained rafters above.

"What's wrong, Maggie?" Kelly's gentle voice broke the silence as she smoothed Maggie's wet, tangled hair, her fingers speaking the sympathy her words couldn't convey. "Are you still feeling sick? Should I take you back to your mother?"

The blankness in Maggie's eyes softened. Her mouth twisted into a sorrowful curve, her lower lip trembling like a leaf in a gust of wind. She turned her face down and began to sob uncontrollably. Kelly pulled her into a tighter embrace, trying to comfort her distressed friend. Nearby workers overheard the heart-wrenching sobs, their hands losing their usual dexterity as they assembled the boxes, yet they didn't dare approach or voice their sympathy.

"I'm so sorry, Maggie," Kelly whispered. "Don't cry like this; you'll see things will get better eventually."

"Mom's gone," Maggie blurted out. Kelly was speechless, unable to find any words of consolation. How could you comfort someone who's lost their mother? Maggie explained that her mother, bedridden with tuberculosis for the past year, was now lying alone and uncared for at home.

"I loved her so much, I didn't want her to die," she said with heartbreaking simplicity. "I was terrified to go home after work, fearing she'd be dead when I got there, and I was scared to sleep at night, thinking she might pass while I slept. She lay so still, and looked so pale and lifeless... I would prop myself up on my elbow and watch her, terrified that her next breath would be her last."

I prayed constantly, pleading, "Oh God, save her! Oh God, have mercy!" But the words stuck in my throat, and I'd swallow hard to hold back the tears. I watched her intently, my heart filled with dread. Whenever the uncertainty became too much, I'd gently touch her with my foot to check if she was still warm, which would wake her, and I'd feel so guilty for disturbing her rest.

"All last night, I kept my eyes on her face," Maggie continued through her sobs, tears streaming down her cheeks, while Kelly wept silently alongside her.

"She wouldn't touch the food I brought, and when I spoke to her, she didn't seem to understand. She kept talking about Father, who's been gone for so long, and sometimes she laughed, which only made me cry harder. It was like she couldn't even see me. Whenever I tried to speak to her, she would start talking about something else from the past. So, I just watched and watched. I couldn't find the strength to pray anymore; all the words had left my soul. Just before dawn, she grew very still. Sometimes a harsh, rolling sound would come from her throat, and when I tried to give her water, she couldn't swallow it. Finally, I couldn't bear it any longer. I cried out to her, 'Mother, mother, please speak to me. I've always loved you, please, just once!' Her lips moved, and I leaned in, holding my breath, desperate to hear her. She whispered, 'Lucille, my pretty one,' then her eyes opened, her head fell to one side, but she didn't see me. She was gone, truly gone, without a word for me, and I loved her so much."

Kelly Morgan shared what little food she had with Maggie that day. The grief- stricken girl kept working, determined to earn some money to help bury her mother with dignity.

That afternoon, foreman Flint strode in and, with a swift motion, pinned a notice to the elevator shaft. He barked at the girls to read it, vowing they'd learn not to disobey again and promising they'd work even harder next week. Fearful and anxious, the girls gathered around the shaft, their dread palpable as they anticipated more bad news. Their suspicions were confirmed at first glance: a pay cut. Tears welled up in some eyes, while Kelly, the boldest and strongest among them, spoke out passionately against the injustice. They were already earning less than their peers in other factories.

"There has to be justice for us just like there is for men, if we only demand it," she declared, rallying them. "Let's stand up for our rights. We'll all go down together, and I'll tell the boss we can't survive on this reduced pay. If he agrees to our old wages, we'll come back. If not, we strike."

The more courageous girls eagerly supported the plan, and the more hesitant ones followed, unsure of what else to do and intimidated by their own audacity. Kelly Morgan, holding little Margaret Williams's hand, led the way. The girls marched quietly after her, two by two, descending the nearly vertical stairs. Kelly paused in front of the frosted glass door on the first floor, which bore the inscription:

.... Archie Stammen, . PRIVATE. .
....

Her heart pounded, but with a firmer grip on Maggie's hand, she pushed the door open and stepped inside.

CHAPTER FIVE

A rchie Stammen Was Deep In Conversation With Foreman Flint When Kelly Walked In Through The Door. Stammen Lifted His Head, But Instead Of Noticing Her, He Was Struck With Horror At The Sight Of Maggie Williams's Tear-stained, Swollen Face. He Went Pale And Trembling, His Voice Barely A Whisper As He Gasped, "why Have You Come To Me?"

Margaret's small, grey eyes stared blankly at him in response. Kelly, taken aback by Stammen's reaction, quickly explained that she was representing the other girls he employed. They had decided to appeal to him not to enforce the proposed pay cut, as they were already earning less than workers in other factories. As she spoke, a bizarre look of relief washed over Stammen's face. With a nervous laugh, he sat back down.

"Get out of here," he snapped. "If you don't like my wages, leave them for those who do."

Without even facing the girls again, he began to organize the papers on his desk. When Kelly started to plead for fair treatment, he calmly ordered Foreman Flint to "remove these young women."

"If you dare touch me, I'll kill you!" Kelly shouted, her eyes blazing with a fierce intensity. Flint, taken aback, froze and stammered an excuse. He feared the fire in Kelly's eyes and chose to heed her warning. Mr. Stammen, moving quietly to the door, held it open and said mockingly, "Careful, my beauty. That fierce spirit of yours could get you into trouble one day."

Kelly shot him a scornful look as she and Maggie exited, and the door closed behind them. Outside, Kelly informed the waiting girls about their failure, and they all headed home, promising to return on Monday to prevent others from taking their jobs. Surprisingly, the girls seemed to embrace the extra holiday, feeling the weight of their decision far less than Kelly did.

That evening, Kelly sold all her furniture and extra clothes. The money she got, combined with her savings, went towards saving Mrs. Williams' body from ending up in Potter's Field. It still wasn't enough to cover the undertaker's fees, so Kelly had to borrow the rest from Blind Gilbert, the beggar who lived in the room behind the Williamses.

Monday morning, the factory entrance was crowded with girls, urging the new applicants not to take the jobs and thereby harm the ongoing strike. Only the foreign workers refused to heed their pleas. They applied for and got the jobs the strikers had left behind. By Tuesday, even more foreigners were hired, causing some of the weaker strikers to panic and go back to work. This infuriated the loyal strikers, who waited for the deserters that evening as they left the factory.

Attempts at persuasion quickly escalated into a brawl. Kelly Morgan, acting as a picket further down the street, rushed over to calm the fighting, sobbing girls. Just then, Foreman Flint arrived with a police officer in tow. With a sinister grin, he singled out Kelly and instructed the officer to arrest her. The frightened girls recoiled as the officer seized Kelly, ignoring her protests.

She spent that night in a cell at the station-house. The next morning, she was taken to the Essex Market Court. The judge, swayed by the officer's embellished tale, asked Kelly for her side of the story. Despite her attempts to explain the truth, he dismissed her with "ten days or ten dollars."

Penniless, Kelly was sent to the Island, enduring the most miserable ten days of her life. When she was finally released, it brought neither happiness nor relief.

She knew going back to her empty apartment was pointless; the rent was overdue and there was no one to help her. Margaret Williams, her only friend, had her own struggles keeping afloat. Feeling disheartened, broke, and hungry, she spent the day drifting from place to place, begging for any sort of job. Everywhere she went, the response was the same: too many workers, no openings.

As night fell, she thought of the Christian shelters, supposedly sanctuaries for the desperate. She tried several on Second Avenue and Bleecker Street, but found no solace. They were either full or turned her away because she wasn't religious and had stopped going to church long ago. The final place, where they asked no questions about faith, wanted twenty cents for a bed. Exhausted and starving, she was forced to head back into the night, rejection stinging her soul.

Eventually, she spotted an open door leading to a dispensary on Fourth Avenue. She slipped into a dark corner of the hallway, where she spent the night. Come morning, she managed to get a glass of milk and a cup of broth from the diet kitchen before resuming her futile search for work. The city was indifferent; her efforts bore no fruit. Tired and despondent, she wandered aimlessly until she reached the Park.

The shade of the trees offered some comfort, and she watched the cheerful passersby, their laughter contrasting sharply with her despair. The more she observed their happiness, the deeper her sorrow grew. Life seemed full for them, but empty for her. As dusk approached and the Park emptied out, her sense of isolation intensified. She had nowhere to go, no one to care for her, nothing to hope for.

Lost in her thoughts, she ventured deeper into the Park. The idea of eternal rest began to seduce her. The notion of a long, painless slumber without hunger or sorrow seemed like a blessed escape. She noticed the reservoir and climbed up, peering into the dark water below.

The dark waters stretched out before her like a smooth, seamless blanket, and the surrounding rugged landscape seemed to push her toward the comforting escape it offered. An overwhelming sense of peace filled her, banishing her exhaustion and wrapping her in a soothing calm.

"'Rest, eternal rest,' echoed softly in my mind," Kelly finished her story, eyes brimming with an unusual serenity. "And with a cry of relief, I moved to dive in."

Steve interrupted, his voice firm yet gentle. "I stopped you from making a very rash move," he said. "My dear, there are countless compassionate souls in New York, ready to help those in need. There is kindness and faith out there."

"That sort of help is rare," Kelly sighed. "And it's almost never found in those so-called shelters."

"Here's what we're going to do," Steve declared, striking a match to check his watch. "First, we find something to eat because I'm starving. Then, if you'll show me the way, I'll take you to your friend Maggie Williams. We'll see what can be done for someone who's quick to surrender."

Steve inwardly questioned the girl's tale. He didn't want to rush to a conclusion, though. If she had indeed endured what she described, not only would he willingly assist her, but his sister Stephanie would be thrilled to brighten the life of someone battered by fate. So, he resolved to escort her to Margaret Williams, if she existed, and find out the truth from there. Steve demonstrated considerable prudence for his age. If it turned out to be a genuine call for charity, he'd be the first to offer support. But skepticism lingered.

CHAPTER SIX

In A Small Oyster Bar Near The Park, Steve And Steve Managed To Find Something To Eat. Steve Also Realized He'd Saved The Life Of A Stunningly Pretty Girl. Normally, Steve Collins Would Have Turned His Nose Up At A Meal In A Place Like This. But Tonight, He Not Only Ate But Enjoyed It. He Didn't Even Pay Attention To The Unappealing Appearance Of The Hefty German Waiter. When They First Arrived, The Waiter Had Brusquely Leaned On The Table With Both Hands And Said With A Thick Accent, "beer?"

Using a grimy towel, the waiter wiped down the sticky spots on the table while Steve ordered dinner from a menu that looked like it had served as flypaper in a previous life. The waiter stepped out after taking the order, shutting the door carefully behind him. The room was evidently meant for small gatherings, as it contained only a table and four chairs.

"Don't you think it's too warm in here?" Steve asked. Without waiting for a response, he got up and flung the door wide open. The waiter returned, covering the table with a thin cotton napkin and setting down pickles, crackers, salt, pepper, and two tiny pats of butter, each the size of a half dollar, then brought over the clams. Once done, he left again, carefully closing the door behind him. When Steve called after him and got no response, Steve opened the door himself. Kelly Morgan gave Steve an innocent, questioning smile. She had no idea Steve had any reason for opening the door other than to cool the room down.

The waiter returned once more and shut the door again. Steve's face flushed with anger as he sternly said, "I want that door open. Leave it that way."

The waiter gave an insolent, almost familiar grin but left the door open for the rest of their meal.

As Kelly Morgan sat across from Steve, delicately savoring her meal, her cheeks began to glow with a warm, lively hue. Her brown eyes sparkled like sunlight dancing on a tranquil, dark pool. Her damp hair, loose and curling playfully around her wide brow and pale neck, evoked a sense of artistic beauty. There was something so genuine, so sincere, about her demeanor, and her eyes held a startled innocence that stirred something deep within Steve—an interest he had never felt for anyone but Stephanie. By the end of dinner, Steve had begun addressing her as "Miss Kelly" and then simply "Kelly," without a hint of objection from her. Moments like these tend to dissolve pretentious boundaries and superficial formalities. They had both stared death in the face, and in those harrowing moments, all pretense had been swept away by raw human connection.

They rode down to Mulberry Street in a coupé, and if this was an unusual experience for Kelly, who Steve had rescued, she masked it well with an air of ease that suggested it was second nature.

"That's where Maggie Williams used to live," she pointed out as they turned onto Mulberry Street. Steve leaned forward, but in the dim light, he could make out little of the surroundings.

"She might have moved by now," Kelly continued, a trace of uncertainty creeping into her voice, momentarily shaking Steve's already tenuous faith in her. "She was there when I left, but life changes quickly among the poor."

"Don't stop the driver," she urged hastily, as Steve knocked on the glass with his walking stick. "Drive on to the corner. A carriage stopping here would draw too much attention, and you don't want that."

"Why?" Steve asked, intrigued.

When he couldn't see her face, he liked her less.

"Well, you don't quite fit in this neighborhood, and if you stand out, it might get pretty uncomfortable for a sophisticated guy like you at almost midnight," Kelly Morgan said with a light laugh. Then, seizing control of the situation, she opened the door of the taxi and called the driver to stop. No sooner had Steve dismissed the driver than he regretted it. The old mistrust of the mysterious girl crept back, and he recalled stories of cunning women and the traps they set for their victims. He felt foolish for coming here at night but was too ashamed to turn back.

The warm night had driven many people out of their tenements, seeking a breath of air. Dark groups of silent men and women filled the doorsteps, basement entrances, and curbstones. The unsavory characters who passed by offered little comfort to Steve if he were indeed walking into an ambush. There were no policemen in sight, even though he knew the police headquarters was not far away. Quietly, he walked beside the girl, who had also fallen silent. He refused to confess his fears, determined to face whatever awaited him, even if it meant death, rather than show weakness and retreat.

The girl entered the doorway of a dark, run-down building, the only one without a loiterer—a fact that raised Steve's suspicions further. With many misgivings and a pounding heart, he stumbled on the step as he started to follow. Had he made the right choice by trusting this clever girl? Before he could decide, she caught his hand and led him into the dark hall.

A fleeting, troubling thought darted through his mind: holding his hand was surely part of a scheme to leave him defenseless. Desperately, he reached out with his free hand. The moment it made contact with a man's coat and a warm, pliant body, a jolt of horror surged through him like an electric charge.

CHAPTER SEVEN

"Did you bump into something?" Kelly asked, feeling Steve startle beside her.

"It's just me," boomed a deep, reassuring voice. The honesty in its tone erased Steve's fear and nervousness in an instant.

"All good," Kelly replied cheerfully, coming to a stop and knocking on a door. Steve recognized the sound, though he couldn't tell door from wall in the pitch darkness. Someone inside opened it, revealing the outline of a young woman against the light, and a surprised exclamation escaped her lips. "Why, Kelly!"

They stepped inside, and the girl swiftly set about arranging chairs for her visitors.

"Mr. Collins, this is Margaret Williams," Kelly introduced, then turned to Maggie, "Mr. Collins has been really kind to me."

"We were worried about you," Maggie said, warmth emanating from her eyes as she looked at Kelly. "I heard you got into some trouble at the shop. I tried to find you, but neither the station-house nor your home had any information."

"You probably know," she continued, "the girls went back. The strike is over. They wouldn't take me back, so I'm helping out Blind Gilbert. He handles the rent and takes care of the groceries."

In a few straightforward words, Kelly recounted her ordeal since the arrest, not skipping her desperate attempt to end her life and Steve's timely intervention. Meanwhile, Steve surveyed the modest room. A simple table covered with a worn bit of oilcloth stood at the center, with everyone now seated around it. The room was dimly lit by a small oil lamp, its broken chimney patched with a scrap of paper. Discreetly, Steve slipped a bill under the newspaper left on the table where Margaret had tossed it when she opened the door.

A small stove stood close to the wall, with a tin coffee pot and an iron tea kettle, the latter sporting a broken spout. Above the stove, a little shelf held a jar of tallow candles and some upturned flat-irons. The bed, looking precarious and uncomfortable, was covered with a brightly colored calico patchwork quilt arranged in a pattern unlike anything Steve had ever seen or imagined. Several carpet remnants lay haphazardly on the floor, and a much-worn blanket was draped over two nails to serve as a makeshift curtain.

Steve's heart ached at these evident signs of poverty. A deep protective instinct surged within him. "I hope you'll let me help," he said as the girls, having finished their confessions, fell silent. "I believe I can secure a better position for Miss Kelly within a few days."

As he spoke, a tentative knock came at the door. Maggie sprang to open it.

"I just thought I'd drop by to see how you were doing, Maggie," said a deep bass voice from the dark hallway. The voice belonged to a tall, lanky man who awkwardly held a soft black felt hat in his large, reddened hands. His rough clothes hung loosely about him, and he held one shoulder higher than the other, as if to apologize for his towering height. His unruly, dust-colored hair seemed determined to defy any semblance of order, while his red mustache and chin whiskers bristled even more defiantly. Shaggy eyebrows overhung modest blue eyes that seemed to wish they could hide beneath as a turtle withdraws its head into its shell. He greeted Kelly bashfully, and she introduced him to Steve as "Mr.

Martin Shanks, who lived with some friends upstairs, stepped forward and offered his large hand to Steve.

"Nice to meet you, sir!" he said, his face glowing red.

"We bumped into you in the hallway earlier, right?" Kelly inquired.

"Yes, I was standing there when you arrived," Martin responded slowly, casting a cautious glance at Maggie. Maggie looked down, and Kelly was surprised to see her blush. She would have been even more startled if she'd known that this burly man had been keeping watch outside Maggie's door every night since her mother passed away.

"I'm guessing you're not from around these parts," Martin remarked to Steve, his eyes narrowing with suspicion.

"You guessed correctly," Steve answered pleasantly.

"And what line of work are you in?" Martin pressed, nervously fidgeting with his hat.

"Down here, or my job in general?" Steve asked, snapping to attention.

"What do you do for a living?"

"Ah, I get it. I'm a lawyer," Steve replied smoothly.

"A lawyer, huh? And I reckon you're not married, or you wouldn't be spending time with this orphan girl."

"You've got it all wrong," Maggie interrupted, alarmed. "Kelly was in trouble, and Mr. Collins found her and brought her here."

"Martin should mind his own business," Kelly exclaimed indignantly. "If this were my house, I'd show him the door."

"Not on my behalf," Steve interjected warmly. "If Mr. Shanks is a friend of the family, he has a right to know why a stranger is here."

"These young ladies, sir," Martin explained, visibly worried, "they don't have any parents looking after them. When Mrs. Williams passed away, I promised myself I'd make sure nothing bad happened to them as long as I was around."

"That's very kind of you, Mr. Shanks," Steve replied sincerely. Then, bidding the girls goodnight, he left. Martin, still intent on ensuring the stranger left the area safely, walked with Steve as far as Broadway. Steve didn't mind the company; in fact, he appreciated it.

CHAPTER EIGHT

When Steve Next Visited Mulberry Street, It Was To Inform Kelly Morgan About A Job He Had Lined Up For Her With A Well-known Photographer. Her Role Was Straightforward And Pleasant—she Would Be Managing The Reception Area. Kelly Was Thrilled; It Seemed Perfect For Her. Before Her Father Passed Away, She Had Spent Countless Hours Immersed In Sketching, And This New Position Felt Like A Step Back Towards That Cherished Past.

While Steve conversed with the girls, he heard a soft scraping sound from the hallway. Soon, the door creaked open, revealing an elderly man with a pronounced stoop, almost to the point of a hunch. Using his cane to navigate, he carefully made his way inside and shut the door behind him. A small, spotted dog with a short tail and boundless affection trotted alongside him, its body wriggling with joy.

"Maggie, are you ready for me and Fritz?" he asked tentatively.

"Yes, Gilbert," she replied gently, guiding him to a chair by the table.

"The young man who has been so kind to Kelly is here," she added, and the old man's face lifted with interest, as if he longed to see.

Steve, with thoughtful sincerity, stepped forward and warmly clasped Gilbert's trembling hand.

"I'm pleased to meet you, sir," Blind Gilbert said respectfully. "Maybe you've heard of me. I've had a stand on Broadway for sixteen years now. I don't do much business, but I'm grateful for what I have. The Lord, in all His mercy, saw fit to afflict me, but He never let old Gilbert starve."

"How did you lose your sight?" Steve asked clumsily, not wanting to comment on the supposed mercy behind such a misfortune.

"Well, it happened very suddenly."

I had a little shop in this very room, sir, and I lived in the back room ever since I lost my business. I had done well for myself since my wife and I moved from Ireland, some forty years ago. My wife fell ill, and after racking up a hefty doctor's bill, she passed away. God bless her soul—though we had our disagreements, she was a good woman to me. One morning, right after she had been laid to rest, I stepped out to cross Mulberry Street. The sun was shining brightly, making it a beautiful morning. But halfway across the street, everything went pitch-black, and I cried out for help. They took me to a doctor, but he said I had gone blind and there was nothing he could do. After some time in the hospital, I could see some light with one eye, but that too faded, and they confirmed there was no hope for my sight. I couldn't stand being cooped up, so I returned here. My shop was gone and everything with it, so I got a license and went down to Broadway to beg. Eventually, I saved enough to rent this back room again, and here I've stayed ever since.

"Does what you get cover all your expenses?" Steve asked.

"The city gives me forty dollars a year. I manage to scrape by with that," the old man replied.

Maggie lifted a newspaper off the table, revealing a simple meal beneath it. She took some fried steak and potatoes from the oven and placed them before Gilbert. Steve felt a bit out of place and started to leave, but they urged him so warmly to stay that he finally sat back down. When Maggie poured Gilbert's coffee, she offered some to Steve as well. Not wanting to offend her, Steve accepted the thick cup gratefully.

The coffee was the worst Steve had ever tasted. Though he tried to mask his distaste, his face betrayed him, stiffening as he forced the vile brew down his throat.

"Want another cup? This one's warmer," Maggie offered as Steve finally set his cup down.

"No, thank you," he said firmly, his voice thick. Maggie eyed him with concern, while Steve, caught in the awkward moment, blushed. Struggling with the gritty remnants of coffee grounds, he discretely used his handkerchief to rid himself of them and reassured her.

"I never drink coffee before dinner," he explained earnestly. "I only made an exception because you prepared it."

He managed a smile, though it didn't quite reach the warmth he intended. Maggie blushed nonetheless. Fritz, the speckled dog, gorged his food with the urgency of a traveler at a station, then sidled up to Steve, seeking affection.

"Fine dog, Fritz," Blind Gilbert noted, hearing the canine's movements. "Gettin' on in years, like me. Maggie, she's my adopted daughter—I never had kids of my own. If you're ready, girl, we'll head to my shop."

Maggie put on her hat and attached a leash to Fritz's collar. She gave Steve a small smile, then took Gilbert's hand to lead him out.

"She's quite worried about her sister Lucille," Kelly confided to Steve once they were alone. "Lucille left two weeks before Mrs. Williams died and hasn't returned."

"Did she say how long she'd be gone?" Steve asked, feigning interest. He was growing tired of delving into the troubles of young women.

"No, and that's the baffling part," Kelly replied eagerly. "They had no clue she wasn't coming back."

"Do they know where she went?"

"Not a clue."

"She said she was going out to pick up some extra work."

"What kind of work?" Steve asked, his curiosity piqued.

"She was a typist and a stenographer," Kelly explained. "In the evenings, she'd take on additional jobs to make ends meet. But this time, when she went out, she didn't come back. Naturally, Maggie's worried sick."

"Who wouldn't be?" Steve replied with genuine concern. "Did Maggie talk to her sister's employer? Maybe he could shed some light on what happened."

"She did," Kelly nodded. "Her boss said Lucille had requested a two-week vacation, which he approved. Maggie didn't want to tell him Lucille was moonlighting, worried he wouldn't take kindly to it. He paid her weekly and had no idea she was taking on extra work. At first, Maggie thought Lucille would just come back when her vacation was over, but now it's been five weeks, and there's still no sign of her."

"And our mother loved her so much," Maggie added, her voice thick with emotion as she re-entered the room. She had just returned from dropping off Blind Gilbert at his usual spot.

"Do you think we could do anything to find her?" Kelly asked eagerly.

"I'm not sure what else there is to do, aside from notifying the police and posting missing person ads," Steve replied, a hint of weariness in his tone. His hands were already full, juggling concerns about Stephanie, the enigmatic Park Mystery girl, and now Kelly. Adding Lucille to the mix was almost too much to think about.

He took a deep breath, feeling a sense of satisfaction in looking after Stephanie, but was clear that he didn't want any additional responsibilities.

"I'd bet she's gotten a better job somewhere and you'll hear from her soon," Steve said, trying to be reassuring.

"If that were true, surely she would have sent for her clothes by now," Kelly responded anxiously. "Tell us what we should do, and we'll do it. Maggie is so desperate to find her."

"I can handle everything for you," Steve assured. "If you give me a detailed description of her, I'll forward it to the police, and they'll start looking for her."

"She was slender, with a lovely fair complexion, blue eyes, and black hair," Kelly began as Steve took notes diligently.

"Was she tall or short?" he asked, pausing to let Kelly respond.

"She was about my height, don't you think, Maggie? I'm five feet four and a half inches."

"How was she dressed?" Steve prompted.

"She was wearing a black alpaca dress and a small black turban with a bunch of green grass on the back," Kelly described.

"And she took her light jacket with her because Mom thought it would be cold on the way home," Maggie added, helping Kelly. "Lucille always had nicer clothes than I did. She was twenty-one, but looked younger. I'm older than she is."

CHAPTER NINE

S teve Collins Reported Maggie Williams' Missing Sister To The Police And Placed A Carefully Worded Yet Enticing Ad In All The Major Newspapers, But Lucille Remained Missing, With No Trace Of Her To Be Found.

"God, what a curse it is to be poor," Steve thought aloud as he strolled up Broadway one morning. "Every visit to Mulberry Street gives me a heartbreak, seeing the struggles people face. Take Gilbert, for example—blind and helpless, forced to sit on a Broadway corner begging for scraps. He sits there, waiting for pennies, yet, he clings to life as if he owned a fortune. And those women down there, with their crying, dirty kids, stuck in garrets and cellars. What are they living for?

"They've got no joy, no happiness, no comfort, and yet they're raising families to endure the same miserable conditions. It's just brutal.

"Then there's Maggie and Kelly. They live in that miserable, God-forsaken room. No fancy dresses, no jewels, no treats for them. But despite everything, they're more cheerful than any girls I know on the Avenue. Kelly's found some work now, and Maggie would be happy too if not for her missing sister. I have to hand it to them—I respect their spirit. And I'll find Maggie's sister, come what may. Solving the mystery of two girls isn't any harder than solving the mystery of one," he thought with a touch of grim humor, given his lack of progress.

"I wouldn't be surprised if Maggie's sister, sick of living in poverty, found herself a better setup and decided to stay. If only I knew what she looked like, I might come across her in my rounds. New York feels like a small place when you're always out and about."

If I knew that girl and she was out and about, I'd bet good money that I'd run into her within three nights. If only I could identify her! Wait a minute, I've got it. I'll enlist Kelly—she knows the girl. I'll bring her to all the spots where we're likely to encounter the missing sister. Why didn't I think of this sooner? If I don't uncover everything about her within a week, well, I'll find that little rascal, that's all.

Boosted by his new plan, Steve cut across Twenty-fourth Street and entered the Hoffman House bar. Without stopping, he made his way to the office, where he scribbled and sent a note to Kelly, inviting her to dinner that evening. He then strolled back to the bar, basking in his decision to embark on this promising path. Steve stood before the famed counter, noting how daylight drained the room of half its allure. The usual crowd—the worldly men, the fashion plates, the extravagant youth, the bejeweled actors, and the shady characters whose lives couldn't withstand scrutiny—had all vanished with the night. The Flemish tapestries appeared lackluster, and the once-stunning Eve statue seemed a muted white, having gained a sudden modesty. The nymphs and satyr appeared worn out and lifeless.

What a contrast to the evening hours, when the gaslights made the cut-glass pendants on the chandeliers sparkle with vibrant colors, and the entire setting seemed lively and animated. Now, everything was dormant. The bartenders seemed dull and disinterested, and a solitary man at the bar drank as if he had nothing better to do. He was a stocky fellow, well-dressed, with a black beard and mustache. His small, sharp eyes, peering over his high nose, critically surveyed the handsome and affable Steve.

He set down his empty whiskey glass and, after a sip of ice water, remarked in a flat, emotionless voice, "Pardon me, but do you know you're being watched?"

Steve laughed lightly. "I knew they were on my trail a few days ago, but I thought they had given up. What do you know about it?"

"I saw a guy shadow you to the office when you got here, and he followed you when you left. He slipped out the side door right behind you. He'll be watching when you leave again," the man continued, still detached and indifferent.

"Thanks," Steve said, grateful for the heads-up. "It's nice of you to warn me about him."

"The game was too easy if you didn't know," the stranger replied with a sly grin. "I just wanted to make the guy work a bit, earn his pay. Now you can both be on your guard."

"Thanks," Steve repeated, absently. He sensed that the stranger's warning carried more malice than goodwill, but quickly felt guilty for doubting his intentions.

"If you want to see who he is, I'll walk out with you and point him out," the man offered roughly, a glint in his eyes hinting that the potential tension between the two amused him.

"Thank you. Care to join me for a drink first?" Steve asked. "Whiskey," he called to the bartender. "I really appreciate your help. If I can ever return the favor, just let me know," he said, pulling out his card case and handing over a card as they both raised their glasses. The stranger glanced at the name and turned deathly pale.

The glass slipped from his lifeless grip, shattering against the hardwood floor. He braced himself against the solid mahogany bar, seeking stability in its timeworn surface.

CHAPTER TEN

One Evening, Mr. Steve Collins Discovered A Letter Waiting For Him As He Arrived Home To Prepare For Dinner.

"Washington, June 3rd, 18—

Dear Steve,

I'm relieved to tell you that our extended visit is finally ending, and tomorrow we head back to New York—to you. I wonder if we've been missed. I'm eager to see you and hear all about the poor girl who died.

I can't shake how I feel about her. Auntie thinks I'm morbid and depressed. At night, when I close my eyes, I see her there again: her golden hair, her small, delicate hands, her fine clothes. I lie awake, wondering whose beloved daughter she was, how she ended up so far from home, and why no one ever found her.

I'm convinced she eloped with some rogue who eventually tired of her and murdered her to escape.

When will you uncover the truth behind this tragic mystery?

Your short, cryptic letters have felt like mere distractions, shielding me from the astonishing story you're saving for me.

If you've been wasting time chasing after the many girls who used to catch your eye, rather than focusing on the Park mystery case, I don't think I could ever forgive you.

I forgot to mention in my last letter that we ran into Clara Chamberlain and her mother here. They came for a day to handle some legal matters regarding Clara's Washington property. Clara admitted that the engagement rumors we heard a while back are true. None of us believed them at the time, but it's confirmed, and the wedding is set for the seventh. Auntie is attending, and I promised Clara I'd be there too.

"Isn't this going to be a bit of a shock for your friend Chauncey Osborne?"

"Her fiancé, from what I hear, is completely unknown in our circles. Clara has always had a unique way about her, hasn't she? She claims he's charming, cultured, and quite capable—a notable politician poised to make waves."

"Auntie bumped into an old friend here, Mr. Schuyler, who went to school with her. Seems like they've been reminiscing about their school days—they were childhood sweethearts, and hearing them laugh over their past antics is genuinely heartwarming."

"You know, I'm convinced that girls today don't have nearly as much fun as they did back in Auntie's time. I can't imagine, when I'm her age, sitting down with an old friend to laugh about the mischief we got into as kids. Whenever Auntie and Mr. Schuyler talk, I feel a twinge of sadness for my own more mundane life."

"But look, I've written four times as much as you did in your last letter. Mr. Schuyler is coming with us to New York, and we're going to show him around. He hasn't been there since he was a boy."

"Hope you've been behaving yourself while I've been away. Sincerely, Stephanie."

To Steve Collins, Esq., The Washington Hotel, New York City.

"I almost forgot to mention that Clara's fiancé, I hear, owns a factory which gives him a rather comfortable income. His name is Archie Stammen. Do you know him?"

"The name rings a bell," Steve mused as he folded the letter and slipped it into his pocket. "Yet, I can't recall ever meeting someone by that name. Perhaps it's from reading about Clara's engagement; I'd almost forgotten the whole affair."

Steve Collins couldn't shake a sense of unease. He yearned for Stephanie's return but dreaded it, knowing he had made no headway with the task she had set for him.

He had imagined she'd be pleased with his consideration regarding Kelly Morgan and Maggie Williams. Yet, when she expressed hope that he wasn't squandering his time with girls instead of focusing on his work, he couldn't help but feel uneasy about how she'd perceive his efforts to help those less fortunate.

"Isn't it strange how we form our likes and dislikes?" Steve asked an hour later, as he and Kelly Morgan shared dinner. He refilled the wine glasses beside their plates. "This wine is excellent, don't you think? Let me serve you some spaghetti. I've often wondered why we instinctively like some people and are put off by others when we first meet them."

"Do you recall the story I told you the first, or rather the second time we had dinner, about the guy who warned me at the Hoffman House that I was being followed? Well, I've run into him several times since. I have this peculiar feeling about him. He seems to dislike me. I can't say I like him, but there's this strange compulsion to stay close to him that keeps me from disliking him either. By Jove, I was shocked when he collapsed against the bar that day, looking terribly ill. At first, I thought my name startled him, but he assured me it was a heart spasm, a chronic condition of his."

"What's his name?" Kelly asked, tearing off a piece of bread.

She had been looking better every day since Steve got her that job, and tonight, in her new gray dress, she looked simply enchanting.

"Clark, I said. Pretty sure I asked for him," Steve said with a laugh.

"You never seem to get tired of checking out all these restaurants," he noted, catching the joy in Kelly's radiant smile.

"Tired? No way!"

Her voice barely conveyed the immense happiness these evenings had brought her.

"I thought you'd get fed up with our little quest before we were even halfway done," he said, admiring the soft brown eyes that had once again given him one of those enchanting glances.

"It's been a dream!" she sighed blissfully. "I adore the bright lights, the stylish, happy people, the busy but silent waiters, the crisp white linens, and the exquisite dishes. Oh, people who can dine out all the time must be incredibly happy."

"You wouldn't think that if you were a lonely man," he replied with a smile, "and had to eat out every single day, three hundred and sixty-five days a year, not counting breakfast and lunch. Sometimes I set out in the evenings and just stop on Broadway, wondering where on earth to eat. Delmonico's, St. James, Hoffman—been to them all, time and again. Lunch here, breakfast there, dinner at another spot last night or the night before. Eventually, I end up in some side street, at a cheap joint where the food's so bad it makes me gag, just so I'll have an appetite for tomorrow. I loathe menus so much that I'll spend half an hour just waiting to see what the guy next to me orders and then get the same thing."

"It's maddening not knowing where to eat," he said, exasperated.

"Maybe that's why some men marry," she replied, a playful glint in her eye.

"Not exactly," he muttered, his cheeks reddening.

"Don't the people in these restaurants ever catch your interest?" Kelly asked, noting his silence.

"Not really. Unless someone's being loud or flashy, I just tune them out like they're monkeys in a cage."

"Every place I go, I find someone fascinating," Kelly said, slowly. "Look at that woman over there in the cherry-red dress and hat. See how proud that little man with her seems? I've overheard her boasting about her past triumphs as an actress. Can't you just imagine the stories she has? And look at that slender, dark-eyed girl with her perfectly white brow, rosy cheeks, and golden hair. See how she flirts with that unremarkable man with the huge nose, bald head, and a mustache that seems to have partaken in his entire dinner. I can just see her as a ballet dancer, trying to impress him for his wealth and connections, overlooking his nasal voice and dull personality."

"Interesting," Steve said, giving Kelly a peculiar smile. "My imagination isn't as vivid or kind as yours. What do you make of the group to our left?"

"That poor little man without legs?" Kelly asked, her eyes welling up. "Despite his affliction, he has such a bright, happy face, and look at all those diamonds on his fingers. The large woman beside him, the one looking at him so tenderly—she must love him deeply because of his condition. I'm certain I would."

The couple across from them, although they didn't appear particularly pleasant, seemed to hang on to every word he spoke, showing clear affection for him.

Steve chuckled quietly. "Kelly, I hate to burst your bubble, but that little man, despite his frail and diminutive frame, possesses an extraordinary intellect. He's at the pinnacle of his field and has amassed a fortune through sheer grit and talent. Quite a contrast to us, won't you say? We were born with legs but haven't managed half as much. Honestly, I admire him, but those companions of his—they're not sticking around for his brains or his struggles. They're not that type."

"So what is it then?" Kelly asked, anxious.

"It's all about the money, Kelly. It's a story that repeats at nearly every table here. That's why I don't let my imagination run wild in places like this. You haven't yet acquired the cynical lens that experience has given me. But let's not dwell on that. While we sip our coffee, let's talk about Maggie's sister."

A girl wandered through, trying futilely to sell a mismatched collection of flowers. A black and yellow bird in a cage high above them craned its neck through the bars, its eyes darting around with curiosity before releasing a series of sharp, defiant cries. Steve lit a cigarette and continued.

"I think it's pointless to keep searching for Maggie's sister. We've scoured all the places where I thought we might find her. Honestly, it's a letdown. I was convinced we'd bump into her somewhere, and that you'd recognize her right away. Do you think there's any way you could miss her?"

"No, absolutely not!"

"I'd recognize Lucille Williams anywhere," Kelly replied earnestly.

"My private opinion," she added in a conspiratorial whisper, "is that she got tired of her family and home. She probably found a better situation and wants to keep her location secret. She knows they'd come asking her for help if they found out where she is."

"I can't believe Lucille would be that heartless," Kelly said thoughtfully. "She was definitely vain and loved her fancy clothes, but I don't think she had it in her to be that selfish."

"What were her habits?" Steve asked, leaning forward with interest.

"Habits? You mean her regular routine? In the summer, she used to hit Coney Island and Rockaway with some guys from her work. But once she landed that office job at the factory where we both worked, she settled down. Stopped going out with anyone. When she did go out, it was always to do some side work."

"How did she get along with your employer?" Steve inquired, his brow furrowed. "You mentioned he had a rough reputation."

"Oh, Lucille got along fine with him. I always thought he was awful, but she never complained. She was pretty easygoing, unlike me with my quick temper," Kelly admitted with a sheepish smile.

"Do you know how he felt about her?" Steve pressed.

"Who? Archie Stammen?" Kelly asked quickly.

"Archie Stammen? Why, yes," Steve replied, caught off guard.

"He was the owner, you know. And Lucille was his stenographer," Kelly explained. "I don't really know what he thought of her. Lucille didn't talk much about him, but she seemed to get along well enough."

A heavy silence fell between them as Steve pondered. Archie Stammen—the name of Clara Chamberlain's fiancé. Archie Stammen—the employer of Lucille Williams and Kelly Morgan. And Archie Stammen—the owner of a downtown factory. It had to be the same man.

Could it really be true? Could Archie Stammen, the man set to marry a banker's daughter, actually be in love with Lucille Williams, a struggling stenographer? Could he have convinced her to leave everything behind for him? The thought wasn't shocking to Steve. From what he'd gathered, Lucille had a fondness for things beyond her reach, and it was likely that her employer, keen to her desires, had helped her attain them. But with his wedding approaching, he probably wouldn't offer her any more enticements to stay. If they found her now, she might be all too eager to return to the modest home of her sister.

Still, what if Archie had never been interested in Lucille? It was all delicate and based on conjecture. Steve's understanding was mostly pieced together from fragments and speculation.

"You think Maggie's sister really worked those nights she was missing?" Steve asked Kelly.

"She always came home with extra money, didn't she? That proves it," Kelly answered firmly.

"Did she ever mention Archie Stammen?"

"Never, except to say he had given her more work than usual or something mundane like that."

"Well, I think Archie Stammen knows something about Maggie's sister," Steve said. Kelly gave him a skeptical smile.

"If she's not with him, he can at least tell me where she is. I've got to see him right away. There's no time to waste; in three days, he's getting married."

CHAPTER ELEVEN

Finding Archie Stammen Proved To Be A Challenge. Early In The Morning, Steve Collins Went To The Box Factory, Only To Learn That Stammen Had Left The City Due To Health Issues. The Employees At The Factory Either Pretended Not To Know Or Genuinely Didn't Have Any Information About His Return. However, Steve Was Certain That With Stammen's Upcoming Wedding To Miss Chamberlain On The Evening Of The 7th, He Couldn't Be Away For More Than A Couple Of Days. Steve Resolved To Confront Archie Stammen Before The Wedding To Find Out The Whereabouts Of Maggie Williams's Sister. For Maggie's Sake, He Also Hoped To Convince Her Sister To Return Home.

Meanwhile, Steve aimed to gather more information about the mysterious girl found in the park. He drove to the morgue, where, after some negotiation, he managed to obtain the bundle of clothes the girl had worn. He took the gloves and the gown, leaving the rest of the items with the morgue keeper. From the quality and design of the dress, Steve deduced that it had been crafted at an upscale establishment. His next move was to visit the high-end dressmakers to see if any of them recognized the craftsmanship.

Steve also took the gloves, though they bore no identifying marks. After visiting several glove stores without success, he realized that tracking the gloves was impractical. No store claimed the gloves, and even if they had, it would have been impossible to trace them to the specific buyer.

Undeterred, Steve proceeded with his plan to visit the fashionable dressmakers, though he felt acutely self-conscious walking into the various establishments with the large parcel in his arms.

The women waiting and the customers in the shop eyed him curiously. When he hesitantly asked to see the owner or the manager, he could barely withstand the amused smiles of those eagerly listening in. His mind raced with discomforting thoughts. At first, he imagined they suspected he was having a dress made for a costume party or an amateur play. But even worse was the notion that they might think he had an unhappy wife who had sent him to return a poorly-fitted dress.

The pinnacle of his discomfort came when he displayed the wrinkled gown to the person in charge and asked if it was their creation. They initially reacted with surprise to his unusual request, followed by a polite but clear indignation upon realizing that Steve had no intention of revealing any secrets about the garment's origin. They ushered him out with an air of offended dignity, leaving Steve feeling very small and unhappy indeed. Some laughed openly, with one even cheekily asking if his wife had refused to disclose where she got it.

Most of the dressmakers denied any involvement with such vehemence that Steve began to suspect the dress might be of lower quality than initially assumed and perhaps originated from a less prestigious shop. Not being familiar with the fierce competition among dressmakers, he didn't realize that one rarely praised another's work. By the time he reached the last notable establishment, it was nearly dinner time. There were no customers around, and the staff were preparing to close for the day.

A young woman approached him and politely asked about his business. Upon hearing he needed to see the person in charge, she asked him to wait and soon returned with a man. For the first time all day, Steve felt somewhat at ease.

Steve explained his peculiar request to the man behind the counter, who listened with an air of detached politeness, giving no sign of surprise or curiosity. He needed to trace the origins of the gown he held—to learn who had commissioned it and where it had been delivered. The man took the gown and disappeared into the workroom, leaving Steve to wait in a labyrinth of nerves. For the first time, a glimmer of hope surfaced in his quest to unravel the Central Park mystery. The longer the man stayed away, the more Steve dared to believe he might be on the brink of discovery. Yet, he guarded his optimism, readying himself against potential disappointment.

When the man finally emerged, the gown draped over his arm, Steve braced himself for news.

"This dress was indeed made here," the man confirmed. Steve's heart quickened. "We received a letter with an order for the dress, complete with measurements and over half the payment in cash. The letter noted that the recipient was out of town and that the dress would be picked up in ten days."

"We often fill orders like this for distant customers," the man added. "We make them based on the provided measurements. Exactly ten days later, a messenger boy arrived with an order to settle the remaining balance and collect the dress. He handed over a $100 bill, from which we deducted the rest of the price and gave him the gown and the change."

Steve struggled to maintain his composure. "Do you still have the letter that included the measurements and order details?" he asked, his voice steady but laced with restrained excitement.

"No," the man replied, shaking his head. "The boy insisted on taking the letter back, so I sent it up to the forewoman in the workroom."

She had recorded the order in her log, pinning the letter alongside it, so she sent it down, and I passed it to the messenger.

"Don't you at least have the name and address of the person who ordered the dress?" Steve asked, feeling increasingly disheartened by the way things were unfolding.

"We have just the name—Miss L. W. Smith—but no address. It's unusual for us, but as I mentioned, we have many clients who send us dress orders while they're out of town. Ladies often aren't meticulous about providing addresses, believing that if we've made an outfit for them once, their name alone will suffice to recall their address and details. We keep detailed records, containing all the information about every garment we make. We rely on these when a client omits necessary details."

"Had you ever made a dress for Miss Smith before?" Steve's hope flared slightly.

"We thought we had, but our records revealed measurements for a large woman, while this order was for someone slender."

"I suppose it's futile to ask if you have any idea where the messenger came from," Steve said weakly.

"I don't know, but there's a messenger office a block up where you might check. It's probably a wild goose chase, though; the lady likely enlisted a boy from her district, and as you know, this isn't a residential area. Still, you might as well ask. They might be able to provide some assistance."

"I can tell you when the boy picked up the gown, but that's about all I can do for you," the man apologized.

He carefully packed the gown into a box for Steve, who left the shop feeling a rare sense of optimism since he and Stephanie had stumbled upon the girl's body. Finally, he was chasing a lead. It wasn't much, but it felt promising. At the District Telegraph office, Steve faced a wall of indifference. They initially claimed it was impossible to figure out which messenger might have collected the dress, and even after a half-hearted search, they came up empty.

"I remember now," one of the messengers piped up from the counter. "I was hanging out front, messing around with Reddy Ryan, who was taking some laundry home, when some guy in a carriage pulled up and asked if I'd run an errand. I told him I was already on a call, so he offered me a dime to find him another messenger. I fetched Shorty, No. 313. I remember because Shorty told me the man had just sent him to Moscowitz's to collect a dress and settle a bill, and tipped him a dollar."

"Where's No. 313 now?" Steve asked, his hope rising dramatically.

"He's on a call. Oh wait, here he comes," said the messenger who had offered the clue. "Hey, Shorty, come here. You're needed."

Shorty was a scruffy redhead with a freckled face and only one eye. As the conversation was recounted for him, Shorty nodded his head, confirming he remembered. Steve probed further, asking if there had been a woman in the carriage, but Shorty was certain there hadn't been. Pressing his luck, Steve inquired about the man's appearance, but the best Shorty could offer was that the man had a mustache and wore a soft felt hat.

Steve had no strong opinion about whether the carriage was private or rented, but he figured it wasn't a typical hire, "because the harness made a distinct jingle."

The other, more insightful messenger noted that the man was young, dismissed the idea of a soft felt hat, and declared the carriage to be a rented one. Steve rushed through dinner, gripped by an uncharacteristic sense of happiness, and went to meet Kelly Morgan for one last evening in their peculiar quest to find Maggie's sister. Tomorrow, Stephanie would return home, and he had found a clue—minuscule, perhaps, but a clue nonetheless. This small victory filled him with hope for a successful conclusion. He had discovered where the dress had been made and that a man had collected it. He enlisted the two messenger boys to help him scour the town for the man who had taken the dress the deceased girl was wearing. Once he found this man, the rest would fall into place.

Steve took Kelly to the Eden Musée. After she had explored all the exhibits that intrigued her, he guided her up to a cozy perch above the orchestra, where tall green palms softened the electric light. He ordered ice cream for Kelly and a Culmbacher beer for himself. Lighting a cigarette, he allowed himself to be swept away by the enchanting Hungarian music and dreams of Stephanie. The music wept and sighed, carrying Steve on clouds of reverie, and he felt a serene happiness. He was convinced he would solve the mystery, and then years of joy with Stephanie stretched endlessly before him. How wonderful it was to be happy; life was so fleeting, why should anyone willingly choose unhappiness if they could help it? A profound tenderness filled his heart, a calming peace enveloped him, making him feel incredibly gentle. And poor little Kelly—how bleak her future seemed.

Steve's heart ached with empathy as he gently held the girl's hand, meeting her trusting gaze. Her soft, brown eyes reflected a deep sense of dependency, and Steve felt a surge of tenderness wash over him. As he thought about the happiness and love that awaited him and

Stephanie, his mind turned to Kelly. What future lay ahead for someone as lonely and forlorn as her?

The melancholic music crescendoed into a final, lingering note.
Steve, deeply immersed in the companionship of the doe-eyed girl
beside him, was jolted from his reverie. He lifted his gaze from her
vividly colored face, only to be met by the stark contrast of Stephanie
standing before him. Her face was pale, her eyes hard and unyielding.

CHAPTER TWELVE

T he sight of Stephanie left Steve speechless. He fought the knee-jerk reaction to jump up and greet her, instead sitting motionless as he subtly tried to release Kelly's hand. Stephanie, with a barely noticeable nod of acknowledgment, continued past him, her aunt and a gentleman who, unnoticed, had already walked by with her.

"Damn it," Steve muttered under his breath. Panic gripped his thoughts. "I'm in for it now. Stephanie will never believe that my thoughts of love for her made me feel compassion for this lonely girl. She'll think I was making a move on Kelly just because I held her hand, and she'll never forgive me. What a fool I am, risking a lifetime of happiness with Stephanie, just to show sympathy for someone who's alone. Poor girl. But it's all over with Stephanie now. I saw that look on her face – she won't forgive or trust me again. I might as well give up. The Park mystery isn't worth trying to solve, nothing is."

Kelly appeared uneasy, having witnessed everything and partially understanding the situation. She spoke in a small, strained voice, "I'm very sorry."

"I wish some guy would step on my toes or punch me in the ribs. I just need a reason to bash someone's face in," Steve said, his voice seething with frustration. Kelly let out a soft laugh at his outburst but carefully avoided mentioning the woman who seemed so angry.

"I forgot to tell you," she began after a pause, desperately trying to shift the conversation, "that it's finally all arranged."

"What is?" Steve asked absently, his mind still lingering on Stephanie.

"The affair between Maggie and Martin Shanks. Didn't you know?" she asked, surprised. "I saw it all the first night you brought me back."

Steve turned to her with a touch of curiosity. "I didn't notice anything in particular, but I do remember distinctly bumping into Mr. Shanks in the dark," he said grimly.

Steve always felt a twinge of disgust when he remembered his fears that night, and he couldn't help but hold a grudge against lanky Martin Shanks for being in the wrong place at the wrong time.

"Well, Maggie and Martin are in love," Kelly announced exuberantly.

"Really?"

"Yes, and last night he proposed and she said yes. They're getting married on Sunday and heading to Coney Island for their honeymoon," Kelly sighed dreamily.

"Good for Martin. I wish I were that lucky," Steve replied, half envious, reminded painfully of the end of his relationship with Stephanie. "I should get Maggie a nice present."

"It was all so amusing," Kelly said with a tinkling laugh. "I'm a bit sad their courtship ended so quickly. Martin was so devoted, so shy, and completely smitten. The only time he ever showed some backbone was the night you escorted me home."

"I remember it clearly," Steve said dryly.

"I thought he was quite rude that night, but that's just how he is. He's liked you ever since. He always stood watch in the hall; every night I came home, I would trip over him, but he couldn't be persuaded to come inside. Whenever Maggie took Blind Gilbert to his stand, Martin followed to make sure she got home safely. But if she looked at him or spoke to him, he was too embarrassed to respond."

"He gave her flowers once, and when she thanked him, he was so flustered that he stammered he found them on Broadway and thought she might as well have them. Poor guy had bought them just for her. Then he bought some fabric for a dress, and when Maggie said she couldn't accept it, he claimed he didn't want it either since he had no use for it. Just picture Martin Shanks in a dress!"

Steve chuckled at the image of lanky Mr. Shanks wrapped in yards of floral- patterned fabric.

Shanks in a gown.

"His proposal was hilarious," Kelly said with a laugh. "There was a loud knock on the door. Maggie opened it to find a work-basket. She picked it up, opened the lid, and there inside was a simple gold ring."

"Martin," she called out, walking to where he stood in the hallway, "you're too generous. I can't accept all these things."

"I was kinda hoping the parson who brings us tracts could put that ring on your finger. Then you'd have the right to do my mending. Just a thought, maybe I'm wrong?"

"Then Maggie said gently, 'Come in, Martin,' and he asked, 'If you'll be with me, Maggie?' She blushed, nodded, and said, 'Yes, Martin.' He stepped into the room, saying, 'I'll come in to settle things.'

"When he walked out again, all the plans had been made for a quick wedding. Martin said there was no point in dragging out an engagement, so they're getting married on Sunday. They're the happiest couple you've ever seen," and Kelly sighed wistfully.

"And what about you and blind Gilbert? Are you not part of their paradise?" Steve asked.

"Oh, yes. Maggie says they're going to rent a flat further uptown, with a room for me and Lucille when she returns. Gilbert will stay with them too. It's a pretty big family to start with, but we'll all contribute to the expenses. I don't think Gilbert will move, though. He's fond of Maggie like she's his daughter, but he's been in that house on Mulberry Street for so long that I doubt he'll leave."

"Well, this is our last night to look for Maggie's sister," Steve said, with a touch of regret, "and we haven't had any luck at all."

"I'm sorry for Maggie, though honestly, it might be better if her sister stays away. She wouldn't be a burden on her anymore."

"I plan to meet with Archie Stammen before his wedding and find out where the sister is. If we decide it's the right move, we can convince her to come home. But right now, I've got another important matter that's going to take up all my time. I won't be able to handle Maggie's sister unless Stammen directly tells me where she is when I see him tomorrow. I expect to be too tied up with this big case to see you for a while, but I hope things go well for you. When you get a chance, congratulate Mr. Shanks and Maggie for me."

"Thanking you for all your kindness feels inadequate," Kelly said, her voice trembling.

Steve's blue eyes softened as he quickly replied, "Come on, let's not talk about that. I'm just a regular guy, and if I've managed to help anyone, the pleasure is all mine. I'm thankful you let me believe I've been of some use to you."

"You've been better to me than anyone else," she said passionately, her gaze intense. "You always said gratitude was rare, so I won't mention it. But someday, I'll find a way. I'll show you what you mean to me."

"My dear girl," he said softly, his eyes glistening with emotion, "just be happy. Knowing that will make me happier than anything else."

Kelly looked down, silent. A few tears slipped from her eyes and fell onto her delicate hands, which were folded in her lap.

"Kelly, what's wrong?" Steve asked, alarmed. She lifted her teary brown eyes to meet his, her lips trembling.

He gently took her hands, patting them in a comforting rhythm, not daring to utter a single word.

"They... they would come," she stumbled, her mouth forming a brave smile while her eyes brimmed with tears. "I couldn't stop it."

He remained silent, continuing to pat her hands, feeling a growing sense of awkwardness.

"I was so miserable until you found me, and I've been so happy since then, that I couldn't bear your words."

"I hope I didn't speak harshly," said Steve, who was blind, struggling to grasp her sorrow. In his detachment, he felt he was losing nothing. But she, poor girl, she was losing everything.

"No, that's just it. You are so kind," she faltered. "Please, don't mind me. I'm so foolish, always crying. Don't you think?"

She looked up at him with a sad, small smile that made his heart ache, though he couldn't fully understand why.

"Kelly, will you promise me something?" he asked suddenly.

"Yes," she responded simply.

"Promise me that you'll try to be happy; that you'll never dwell on dark thoughts, no matter what happens. Let misfortune glare at you all it wants. Laugh at it; laugh in its face until your laughter makes it relent. Can you promise me that?"

"Is that what you do?" she asked, evasively.

"Well, I'm not sure. But what does it matter? I don't get as down-hearted as you. Won't you promise?"

"You've brought me happiness. I promise that if I feel blue, I'll think of you. Will that suffice?" she asked, seriously.

"I don't know," he replied, half irritated, but he didn't press further. And these two young people, their paths having run parallel for a brief moment, were beginning to drift apart. Mentally, they were saying their goodbyes, knowing that even if they stayed within sight or call for a few more days, their lives were destined to move in different directions. Silently, they left the spot where they had spent their last evening together and stepped out into the cool, quiet night.

A few dim streetlights flickered along Twenty-third Street, casting a faint glow on the storefronts, which loomed dark and menacing. The occasional passerby emerged from the shadows into the pools of light, only to vanish back into the gloom. A man approached from Sixth Avenue, moving thoughtfully through the still night, like someone seeking solace in the quiet streets due to sleeplessness. Steve noticed him and, gripping Kelly's arm, whispered:

"Check out that guy."

"Yeah, I see him," she replied, a hint of excitement in her voice. As the two men locked eyes, the stranger gave a stiff nod, lifting his hat briefly in response to Steve's friendly greeting. Once they had passed, Steve turned to Kelly and asked:

"Why are you shaking? I just wanted you to notice him. That's Mr. Clarke, the guy I ran into at the Hoffman House bar."

"Mr. Clarke!" Kelly exclaimed, astonished. "That's Archie Stammen!"

CHAPTER THIRTEEN

"Well, this is a surprise," Stephanie Orton said coldly, her eyes narrowing at the sight of Steve Collins. It was the morning after their encounter at the Eden Musée. Steve couldn't stay away, compelled to explain everything about Kelly. He now regretted his decision to keep the affair a secret until Stephanie's return. It only made him seem more suspicious. Stephanie was sharp; she felt the sting of betrayal but had no intention of letting Steve see her pain. She refused to give him the satisfaction of witnessing her jealousy. Instead, she chose a façade of cold indifference, making it clear that whatever he did, it no longer impacted her. She would smile, but without the affection she used to reserve for him. She would make him feel her displeasure and lack of affection without quarreling, offering neither apology nor explanation.

"You don't seem very happy to see me," Steve ventured with a strained smile.

Stephanie looked at him with feigned astonishment, her eyebrows arching, "Really?"

Steve shifted, uncomfortable under her gaze.

"You don't understand," he said, helplessly. "Please, at least let me explain what you saw last night."

Her response came with a frosty smile, "Really, you must excuse me. I have no interest in your personal affairs."

"Come on, Stephanie. Don't be so indifferent," Steve exclaimed, frustration breaking through his composure.

Stephanie's face hardened, her eyes now reflecting pure disdain.

"How's Mrs. Van Brunt?" he asked awkwardly, hoping to defuse the tension.

"Quite well, thank you," she replied, her gaze drifting out the window.

"Is she at home?"

"No; she just went out with Mr.

"Schuyler," Stephanie responded, flipping through the pages of a book without really looking.

"Would it be alright if I visited her?" he asked, his tone detached.

"Auntie would be happy to see you," she replied, putting a strange emphasis on the last word.

"How long are you going to keep up this act, Stephanie?"

She shrugged impatiently, pouting without answering.

"You know, you're being really unreasonable. You're depriving both of us of any chance at happiness. Deep down, you know you never really doubted me. What's the point of pretending? Just stop being so difficult."

"Ha! Why should you care if I'm unreasonable, bad-tempered, or foolish?" she retorted mockingly. "Nice to know what you really think of me. I guess that girl you were with last night is more agreeable."

"Honestly, she might be, Stephanie," Steve said, sounding defeated and out of patience. "I've loved you deeply and put up with all your whims, but if this is how it ends, I can only accept it. If you ever regret this, remember it was your choice. You pushed me away, and I won't come back."

And with that, Steve, feeling utterly miserable, walked out of the room. Stephanie didn't move until she heard the front door close. She expected him to come back; he always had. But when she realized he was truly gone, she was both surprised and a bit scared. Though Steve was usually good-natured, she sensed she had gone too far this time. If she wanted him back, she'd have to swallow her pride. Never before had she lost control like this, and now she felt small and mean-spirited. She couldn't even remember everything she'd said, but she knew she felt deeply wrong.

After losing him, she reflected on her actions and realized that, while Steve had his faults, she had been excessively harsh. He deserved a lesson to prevent future mistakes, but she had been unforgiving. Wasn't Steve always gentle and understanding with her, overlooking her minor faults and whims with tenderness? And wasn't she sure he loved her more than any other woman in the world? So why should she be jealous if he entertained himself with other women who were always eager to catch a man's attention?

A woman in love often blames herself for every fight with her lover. A woman in love tends to fault other women for all the missteps of the man she adores. And this self-reproach continues as long as love endures. While Stephanie spent her day tormented by unhappy thoughts, Steve was busy tracking down Archie Stammen and coordinating with messenger boys to find the person who had paid for the deceased girl's dress. Steve went to Mr. Stammen's office, but was told he was out of town. However, Steve knew better this time. Upon getting the address, he headed to Archie Stammen's bachelor apartment in Washington Square. According to the servant, Mr. Stammen was indeed in town but wouldn't be home until it was time to get ready for a 7 o'clock dinner. The servant didn't know where Mr. Stammen could be found, so Steve had to be content with this scant information until later.

Turning to the directory, Steve found a long list of Smiths, but no Miss L. W. Smith. He decided that if nothing more promising turned up, he would visit the Smiths in the best neighborhoods to personally investigate every family until he found the right one or confirmed that no such Smith lived in New York. He had placed a personal advertisement in all the morning and evening newspapers seeking information about the relatives of Miss L. W.

Smith expected that by evening he'd have a solid lead. His argument with Stephanie hadn't snuffed out his determination to solve the mystery of Central Park; instead, it had ignited a fresh surge of energy. He was now more resolved than ever to crack the case and prove Stephanie's scepticism wrong. With a determined stride, Steve Collins, accompanied by a young messenger, ventured into the heart of the city's hustle and bustle, sticking to his initial plan of scanning the crowd for any familiar faces.

"When you see anyone who resembles the guy who picked up the dress, let me know," Steve instructed the boy. The day turned into a weary shuffle through the city's streets, punctuated by the hope of at least glimpsing the man's face.

"There goes someone who looks just like that fellow," the boy suddenly piped up, as they stood amidst the constant flow of people on Broadway. Steve's eyes followed the boy's pointed finger, landing on a man in the company of another—a red-headed, florid-faced individual carrying an ample share of extra weight. The first man, sporting a light beard, a pronounced nose, and sharp eyes, immediately rang a bell for Steve; he recognized him as an Albany assemblyman.

"That's nothing like the image you described," Steve remarked crossly as they trailed the two into the Hoffman House.

"Well, his face is similar, except the other guy had black whiskers, and this one has red," the boy retorted.

"Probably dyed," Steve said with a hint of sarcasm.

"I'm telling you, he looks the same," the boy insisted. Steve decided to play along and seated himself in the bar-room, feigning interest in a letter. The two men sauntered to the bar, ordered drinks, and as the slimmer of the two (who was still far from thin) raised his glass, something clicked in Steve's mind. That face was definitely familiar.

"I'm done for the day. Head back to the office and meet me here tomorrow," Steve instructed the messenger, who eagerly departed, leaving Steve to chew on his thoughts as the evening's puzzle pieces began to align.

Steve sat there with a somber expression, watching the man at the bar whom the boy had pointed out. He scrutinized him until the man and his burly companion finally left. As the door swung shut behind them, Steve sank into deep contemplation. An outrageous, improbable suspicion gripped his mind—so far- fetched, so ludicrous—that he felt embarrassed to entertain it. The resemblance was uncanny; so different, yet eerily familiar that Steve found himself torn between disbelief and conviction.

"Poor guy! Why should I let a mere similarity make me accuse him of something so awful?" Steve mused. "He already has enough to deal with and answer for. Still... it's just too outrageous, too far-fetched. I need to forget it, push it out of my mind. The messenger must have been mistaken. Tonight, I need to focus on finding Maggie's sister. Here's to an evening free from thoughts of that dead girl. And yet... it's very strange—I almost believe it."

Shaking his head as if to clear away the intrusive thoughts, Steve drained his glass with a sense of finality and headed for Washington Square.

CHAPTER FOURTEEN

Arriving Early, Steve Decided To Pay Kelly Morgan A Visit. She Was Just About To Head Home, And He Invited Her To Stroll With Him Down Fifth Avenue. She Seemed Noticeably Worn Out When He Arrived, But Her Face Lit Up With Pleasure At The Sight Of Him.

"I got a job offer from a theater manager today," she mentioned, her voice steady.

"I hope you didn't take it," Steve responded quickly, noticing her downcast expression, which had changed so much since the previous night.

"Not yet."

"And you won't, right Kelly?" he asked, almost pleading.

"I'm not sure why not, Mr. Collins."

Steve felt a jolt of discomfort. He realized she never addressed him by name before, and now it seemed like she was drawing a line between them. He couldn't help but wonder why.

"I'd be really upset to see you on stage, Kelly. You don't know anything about acting, and it would be years before you could make a name for yourself."

"I **feel** like I can act," she said with intensity. "My nerves are so wound up that I just want to get up there and live out emotions. I want to act out love, then hate, and even murder."

"Why, Kelly?" Steve asked, both curious and concerned, sensing the depth of her emotions. He remembered a remark from an old club member who once said that every woman disappointed in love had a tendency to want to act. He wondered if Kelly had fallen for one of the handsome men who often visited the photo galleries to capture the image of their beloved. Dismissing the thought as unfair, he focused on her.

"I **feel** it, deeply. I can't stand a dull life anymore. I need excitement," she said, her voice quivering with passion.

"You need exercise, Kelly! You need to walk, swing some clubs, and you'll start feeling much better in no time," he suggested.

"You've got so much energy that your job doesn't drain. If you channel it into exercise, you'll be happier and stronger," Steve advised.

Kelly bristled slightly. She hated having her feelings dissected so plainly. They had reached Washington Square now, and she said goodbye to Steve, heading off to her modest home. Steve continued walking along North Washington Square until he arrived at the house where he hoped to find the man who had taken Lucille Williams. He ascended one flight of stairs to Archie Stammen's apartment and knocked on the door, which bore Mr. Stammen's visiting card. In a moment, the door opened, revealing the man he knew as Mr. Clarke.

"Mr. Stammen," Steve said, emphasizing the name, "I need to speak with you privately."

Steve spoke decisively and stepped inside immediately. Mr. Stammen looked as unwell as he had the day he collapsed at the Hoffman House bar. He silently motioned for Steve to follow him into the first room off the hallway. Closing and locking the door behind them, both men entered. Steve sat down in an armchair without waiting for an invitation. Mr. Stammen took a seat at an elaborately carved desk, cluttered with letters and photographs, some of which were slowly smoldering in the open fireplace. The room was impressively furnished, and Steve couldn't help but appreciate its elegance. There was a large open grate, and above the low, wide mantle was a cabinet with a French plate mirror at its center, flanked by fine bits of bric-a-brac. The floor was richly carpeted, the walls adorned with exquisite paintings. Near the drapes, which were pulled back just enough to offer a glimpse of a cozy suite beyond, stood alabaster statues of The Diver and Paul and Virginia. A quaintly colored Mexican serape was draped over a low lounge, in front of which lay a white fur rug.

On one side of the room stood a small, square breakfast table with intricately carved legs. Nearby, a half sideboard, half cabinet showcased an array of elegant dishware: some solid silver pieces and crystal glasses, flanked by long- necked bottles filled with various drinks. Mr. Stammen, having removed his coat and waistcoat, now wore a finely embroidered jacket. His pallor was indeed unhealthy, and Steve couldn't help but notice how Mr. Stammen's hand, which played with a carved paper-cutter, trembled violently.

"This man really loves the finer things in life," Steve mused sympathetically, his eyes drifting from one luxurious item to another. His gaze moved through an open doorway, where he glimpsed a brass cage housing a restless yellow canary, and a small aquarium with a bubbling fountain. Goldfish swam lazily, and a tiny dark turtle poked its head above the water before diving back down to the bottom.

"Do you know why I came to see you?" Steve finally said, noting that Mr. Stammen seemed unwilling to broach any topic.

"No, I can't say that I do," Mr. Stammen replied, feigning indifference.

"Well, I want to know everything about Lucille Williams," Steve said bluntly.

"What right do you have to ask me for such information?" Mr. Stammen retorted coldly.

"Because you persuaded her to leave home," Steve answered firmly, "and I need to know what happened after that."

"I have nothing to tell you," Mr. Stammen said with a faint, sarcastic smile.

"If you won't talk, I'll find a way to make you," Steve said angrily.

"Oh, really?" Mr. Stammen responded, still cool and unconcerned.

"Yes, if you don't tell me what I need to know before I leave, I'll go straight to Miss Chamberlain, your fiancée." Mr. Stammen started uneasily. "I'll tell her a story you wouldn't want her to hear."

"And you think she'd believe you?" he asked derisively.

"I'm certain of it," Steve replied confidently.

"I can prove what I'm saying," Steve declared with unmistakable determination.

"Alright then, go to her. See what you can do."

"By all means, I will. And I'll go to the newspapers too, and I'll tell them—"

"What?" Mr. Stammen asked, clearly uncomfortable.

"You know exactly what! Don't think for a moment that I don't know some chapters of your life that, if made public, will end your monstrous career." Steve hinted darkly, the suspicions that had been simmering within him now crashing over with full force. Archie

Stammen's face twisted in thought. Seeing that his bluff had struck home, Steve resolved to press further.

"Be as nonchalant as you want, Mr. Stammen. Tomorrow, when your wedding is postponed and you are called to answer the serious charges I'll bring against you, you'll regret not taking the easier route and giving me the information I asked for." Steve's voice bore the tone of someone whose patience had run out.

"I don't have any information to give," Stammen replied, his tone revealing his weakening resolve.

"Cut the pretense. Either you will or you won't comply with my request. If not, the consequences will fall squarely on you."

"And would you... do you mean—" Archie Stammen faltered, his confidence eroding under Steve's unwavering resolve.

"Yes, indeed. I mean every word of it." Steve had risen, his anger palpable, an aura of capability radiating from him, promising to carry out every one of his threats. "I've given you a chance, and you refuse to take it, so—" He shrugged, as if to say his responsibility ended there.

"And if you get the information, what will you do with it?" asked Stammen, grasping desperately for some glimmer of hope.

"You know exactly what I want."

"It's not about bringing any credit to myself but about easing the heartache of a devastated sister."

"And if I tell you everything, will you show some mercy?" he asked, a hint of desperation in his voice.

"I can't make any promises. I need a confession before your wedding. If you don't give it, you won't get married. That's a guarantee," Steve said firmly.

"And if I tell you," a spark of hope igniting in his eyes, "will you let the wedding proceed and keep Clara in the dark? Promise to let us leave on our honeymoon, and after that, you can do whatever you want. Just give me that much," he pleaded, visibly trembling.

"And let you ruin the life of an innocent, unsuspecting woman? What kind of man do you think I am?" Steve retorted with disdain.

"For God's sake, man! Show some compassion. Haven't I suffered enough? You're a man, you understand how a man can sacrifice everything for a woman," he said bitterly. "Show some compassion!"

"You can't understand?" he continued, desperately trying to stir compassion in Steve. "She was beautiful, had no friends to defend her, and I lost my mind. I've paid for it. I've regretted it." Archie Stammen covered his face with his hands, and Steve heard a broken, husky sob. The sound was almost more than he could bear. His stern demeanor started to crumble, and he struggled against the urge to console the wretched man. Only thoughts of his impoverished sister kept his resolve intact.

"So, what do you want from me?" Steve asked, his rough tone masking his true feelings. Now that he had secured the confession, his suspicions evaporated. He felt a pang of sympathy for Stammen's suffering and a gnawing guilt for being the cause of it.

"Just give me until tomorrow, and I swear you'll have the information you need before ten o'clock. Give me until then."

"If I fail, you still have time to stop my wedding tonight. You're a man, but if you can't forgive me for my mistakes, do it for the woman I'm marrying. I'm not well! I can't explain any more! Just give me until tomorrow."

"Damn it, Stammen," Steve said with genuine feeling, "if it wasn't for her sister, I'd drop this whole thing." He had no idea what was truly at stake. "I believe you. I'm a reckless man myself, careless as the worst of them, and, hell, I feel for you. Here's my hand."

"Thank you, thank you," Stammen replied, his deep emotions visible in the painful twitching of his pale face. He clasped Steve's firm hand in his own dry, feverish one, squeezing it with gratitude.

"Until tomorrow, then?"

"Until tomorrow," echoed the despairing man, looking into Steve's eyes with such a desperate plea of agony that Steve would never forget.

CHAPTER FIFTEEN

I t was ten o'clock when Steve Collins, wearing a robe and slippers, sat down in a high-backed chair for a light breakfast. The elegant table was laden with fresh rolls, yellow butter chilled with a bit of ice, and crisp, red berries. The tantalizing aroma of coffee filled the air, yet Steve alternated between eating and perusing the morning paper. The lowered awnings blocked the harsh glare of the morning sun, casting a gentle shade into the room. A light breeze stirred the curtains lazily, while a green palm on the windowsill waved its long fronds energetically, as if urging the indolent young man not to miss the early beauty of a summer morning.

Steve Collins's quarters stood in stark contrast to the lavish apartments of Archie Stammen—like a playful child next to a brooding adult. One evoked health and cheerfulness, the other, with its somber tones, hinted at dreams and self- indulgence. Decorated with Rosa Bonheur's masterpieces depicting animal life, pictures of racing horses, and humorous photographs of serious-faced dogs, his room exuded energy and vibrancy. A stuffed fish's head with an agape mouth mounted on a plaque, boxing gloves, clubs, and dumbbells lay scattered, evidence of his sporadic use. An eclectic array of walking sticks, whips, fishing tackle, and firearms added to the charming chaos. The furniture was light, the curtains airy, the carpet bright and soft, a stark contrast to Archie's somber abode.

Steve ate and read, oblivious to the tussle between a bow-legged pug and a cheeky black-and-tan terrier, whose sharp ears stood stiffly, exuding cool amusement at the pug's futile attempts to pin him down. As Steve pushed his chair back and lit a cigarette, a servant entered quietly, placing a large envelope and a smaller one on the table before him. Steve picked up the larger envelope and read the inscription.

"To Steve Collins, Esq. From Personal. Archie Stammen."

He hastily tore it open with his thumb.

The letter got straight to the point:

By writing this, I entrust you with my life. I expect neither mercy nor ask for it. I've been so miserable for days that life has become a burden I can scarcely bear. Do what you will with this information, but if you possess an extraordinary generosity, I ask that you spare me as much as possible after clearing your name.

"My wild, improbable suspicions were correct!" Steve exclaimed, shocked. His black-and-tan dog, hearing his voice, jumped up and wagged its tail inquisitively at his knee. When it received no attention, the dog returned to chewing on the English Kilrain toy on the rug. I first met Lucille Williams when she responded to my job advertisement for a typist and stenographer. Among the many applicants, I chose her. Not because she was the most skilled, but for a man's reason: she had an incredibly pretty face. Wonderfully pretty, as many men had told me. She had large, clear blue eyes, an abundance of wavy black hair, and a flawless pink-and-white complexion that often comes with that combination. Her hands were small and slender, meticulously well-kept, and her remarkably small feet were always stylishly shod.

Life during business hours can be dull, so I amused myself with my attractive typist. It began innocuously, with me playfully putting my arm around her chair while dictating. Harmless enough, yes, but it brought me close enough to her that I began to wonder how she would react if I kissed her. When I paused in my dictation, she raised her big, alluring blue eyes to me in such a way that any man would feel a little thrill of temptation. Eventually, I did kiss her. She wasn't overly offended. She cried a bit and asked what she had done to encourage me to insult her.

Her main flaw was vanity, so I indulged myself and comforted her by holding her close, swearing that her red lips and mesmerizing eyes were simply irresistible. This seemed to soothe her and satisfy me. Yes, I spoke of love; it felt like the only appropriate thing to say in that moment. I'm pretty sure I called her "My Love" and similar endearments. I'm certain I didn't explicitly say that I loved her, though I did coax her into professing her love for me. She said she did, and I believed her. It was all very charming and fascinating as long as the novelty lasted.

We soon began spending our evenings together. I took her to restaurants frequented by the bohemian crowd, knowing anyone we encountered there would be just as eager to keep their visit discreet. In the summer, with fewer chances of running into anyone awkwardly, I took her to more upscale places and sometimes to the theater. It was quite intriguing to me.

During this time, I discovered that Lucille's sister worked at the factory too, and I threatened Lucille with a permanent separation if her family got wind of our relationship. When the excuse of meeting friends or handling business became insufficient, I instructed Lucille to claim she was doing extra work. She sensibly pointed out that she couldn't make this claim without some extra money to back it up, so I made sure she had it. That became her cover. Thus, she kept her family in the dark.

Meanwhile, I thought I'd feel more at ease if Lucille dressed better. You know how men are about this; most would prefer to be seen with the lowest woman in New York, provided she wore a Paris gown, rather than with a woman in rags, even if she were as pure as a saint. A man always dreads being ridiculed for accompanying a poorly dressed woman. The world judges solely by appearance. So, I spoke to Lucille about it.

I discovered that she was just as self-conscious about her inexpensive clothing as I was, so I suggested she buy a complete new outfit that would be suitable for our adventures, and I would cover the cost. I offered some guidance, and the clothes she picked were just as tasteful and appropriate as if she did this every day. Then came the dilemma: where to send the clothes? She couldn't send them home because her mother and sister, despite their poverty, held strict Puritan views about morals and propriety.

There's always a solution to every problem. I arranged for all her new items to be shipped to my bachelor apartment. I then gave her a key so she could come and go as she pleased to change from her old clothes to the new ones. Yes, I did get her to my place. I won't deny that it was part of my plan from the start, but I wanted to maintain the romance of the situation for as long as possible. Lucille was strikingly beautiful, incredibly endearing, and I was eager for our evenings together, wanting to savor every moment of our intoxicating affair.

I won't bore you with the details. You know the sort of freedoms a bachelor pad offers. At first, Lucille was nervous, hesitant to come in or leave, but she quickly grew bolder. She even started to enjoy the thrill of it. I was very fond of her at that time. Let's be honest here, it wasn't love that drove me. I never understood why men use such weak excuses. It wasn't love for her. No man harms a woman out of love for her; it's always love of self. I was fully aware of this, but I was blissfully happy, and happiness is too rare to ignore, regardless of the eventual consequences.

I promised to marry her. It was a pledge made in a moment when I felt my greatest affection for her. Even then, I knew it was a reckless decision.

The next day, I warned her to keep our relationship a secret. There were reasons why, if it became known, it would harm me. Understanding the differences between us, she remained as silent as I could be. Over time, things began to lose their charm. I knew her too well. I grew tired of her pretty face. Her small vulgarities irritated me. She lacked variety and meekly acquiesced to my every demand, which became unbearable. I had known plain women whose appeal was more enduring. Her weakness infuriated me. I grew to hate her. If only she had the spirit to argue with me, but that was the crux of it; she had no spirit until it was too late.

Just before this, I met Miss Chamberlain. She seemed to take a liking to me, and I decided to marry her. It didn't matter much that I wasn't in love; I had long since realized that love was merely a fleeting sensation, akin to music that stirs our emotions but soon fades. I thought it better to marry without strong passion, as such feelings inevitably die, leaving an unbearable emptiness. Without such emotions, there would be no such aftermath to dread.

I didn't anticipate any trouble from Lucille. But I underestimated her. Despite my efforts to keep our engagement a secret, a small note mentioning my impending marriage to Miss Chamberlain made it to the press. Lucille, though not quite a socialite, always read the society pages. She saw the note. She transformed into a tigress, a devil. Isn't it strange how a seemingly weak woman can have such a fierce temper? Expecting nothing more than a few tears from her, I responded indifferently, which only fueled her fury. Naturally, I was astonished.

She accused me of deceit and demanded that I retract the report under my own name and marry her immediately, or she would go to Miss Chamberlain and tell her what she considered my treachery. I was set on getting married. It meant wealth, a better social standing, power, and a wife who would make me proud. Ever since I was a boy, I had aspired to such a marriage, and I was determined that nothing would stop me now that it was within reach. I was resolved to take fate into my own hands.

When I realized I couldn't calm Lucille down, I decided to absolve myself of any responsibility toward her. Call me ruthless if you must! Was I doing anything different from what hundreds of men in New York are doing today? Had my actions strayed any further than those of countless men in the city? You, an educated man of means, judge me if you have never strayed similarly. Let any man of education, leisure, and money in New York judge me, if they themselves have not stumbled in the same way. It was supposed to be a short-lived distraction, harmless if it ended quietly. But I botched it—that's where the real fault lies. Not in my actions, but in my bungling of them.

People can say what they want. My mistake wasn't in my intentions but in my execution. It's the system that's flawed, the system that prevents people who care for each other from being happy while their affection lasts. If the system had been different, Lucille would be at home today, happier and better off than before we met, and I wouldn't be writing this letter to you now. But there was no saving us. Lucille, tired and angry, further irked me with her jealousy and unreasonable demands for a quick marriage. Afraid of losing the marriage that meant so much to me, I carefully planned what seemed like the only viable course of action. Yes, it was deliberate.

Soothing her anger, I convinced her to come to my apartment, the very rooms where I now sit and pen this confession of my crime. Unwittingly, even eagerly, she came, walking right into the trap I had set like a spider's web for an unsuspecting fly.

"Excuse me, sir, Miss Orton's compliments, and she requests you come up as soon as you can," said a voice at the door. The small black-and-tan dog paused for a moment, the pug's ear still clutched between its sharp teeth, to see where the voice originated. Impatiently, Steve replied, "Very well, tell her I'll be there," and turned back to Archie Stammen's letter.

CHAPTER SIXTEEN

The Whole Situation Was A Dark Joke To Me. I Knew Exactly How It Would End, And When Lucille Approached Me With Her Usual Cheerfulness, Completely Unaware That She Wouldn't Be Going Back Home That Night, I Couldn't Help But Laugh. She Wanted To Discuss My Proposal Of Marriage, And I Agreed To Talk. I Quickly Told Her It Was Impossible To Marry Her In Her Current State, But If She Followed My Advice And Bought Suitable Clothing, We Could Then Quietly Elope. To Accomplish This, She Would Need To Stay With Me. She Was Thrilled, Her Eyes Shining With The Prospect Of A Bright Future, But Insisted On Notifying Her Family. Only By Threatening To Call Off Everything If She Let Anyone Know Did I Manage To Dissuade Her. I Did, However, Allow Her To Write A Note Saying She Had Gone Out Of Town For A Few Weeks And That She Would Have A Joyful Surprise For Them Upon Her Return. This Pleased Her And Caused Me No Harm. The Letter Was Never Sent.

Lucille's presence wasn't entirely a secret. My servant, who slept off-site, knew I had someone with me, but he had spent years man-

aging bachelor apartments and was neither surprised nor curious. The
waiters who brought us our meals noticed I wasn't alone, but to them,
it was nothing new and not worth discussing. Nevertheless, I took
precautions to ensure they wouldn't see Lucille. Dressed in the clothes
I had bought her, I sent her to a dressmaker to get her measurements.
I even sent her to a dentist to get some decaying teeth fixed. This was
all part of my plan to free myself from a woman I had grown weary of.
Some might say I could have found a simpler solution, but I couldn't
see how. I was scared of losing my wealthy fiancée and couldn't risk
Lucille spilling everything.

There was a way out through claiming blackmail, which would
have cleared my name. But considering the woman I hoped to marry,
there was no chance I'd risk it. One clear path lay ahead, so I took it.
I had Lucille write an order for a dress from my dictation, specifying
the measurements and arranging for it to be picked up on a set date. I
personally went to multiple stores, purchasing everything needed for
the perfect outfit, sparing no expense. I brought all the items home
in my coupe, ensuring no names or addresses were involved, thus
eliminating any potential trace back to their destination.

During this period, despite her confinement, Lucille was genuinely
happy. She was constantly plotting our future together, eagerly antic-
ipating the sensation our marriage would spark among her acquaintances. She would dream aloud about the best places for us to live, the
furnishings she wanted, and the dresses she planned to buy.

Trying to articulate my emotions during those days would be futile.
I was aware of a deep weariness, driven by a determination not to be
thwarted in my mission. Sympathy for Lucille was absent; I felt largely
detached, neither compelled to help nor hinder her. Her grandiose
visions of our future were almost laughable to me. She would lie awake

some nights, lost in her visions, and I found myself laughing at the absurdity of it all.

I marked each passing night, knowing that with each one, my preparations neared completion. Meticulously, I removed all tags and labels from every item I bought for her. The gloves and suede shoes only bore their sizes.

I removed the crown lining from the hat and, before bringing her dress home, I took out the inner belt stamped with the dressmaker's name. That dress was the second-to-last item I brought to my apartment. I didn't even show myself at the boutique where it was made. I drove nearby, hired a messenger boy, and sent him to retrieve the garment. This way, I kept my identity hidden. The very last thing I bought was a bottle of hair bleaching fluid.

I told Lucille that if her hair were golden to match her eyes, her appearance would be greatly enhanced. She eagerly agreed, always willing to try anything to boost her beauty. Over the next two days, I applied the fluid at regular intervals, and her hair transformed into the most perfect golden shade I had ever seen. It really changed her. Since then, I've marveled at the transformation and admired her newfound exquisite beauty. Yet, I felt nothing beyond a compelling urge to observe her.

I watched her eat, amazed at her appetite. I listened to her light chatter, fascinated by her happiness. I gazed at her while she slept, almost astonished by her apparent sense of security. Why didn't she sense anything? I waited and watched for a sign, any sign, that her instincts would detect the looming end. But there were none. On the last night, I leaned on my elbow and watched her sleep. She looked utterly perfect! Her soft, dimpled arms were thrown above her head, her pretty face nestled in golden hair, her straight black eyebrows, her long, dark lashes resting lightly on her rosy cheeks—all of it destined to vanish into nothing. Tomorrow night, it would all be over; this was her final night. Impulsively, I leaned over her and whispered, "Lucille!"

"Lucille!" I called, but she only opened her big blue eyes, giving me a sweet, innocent smile before snuggling up to my arm, which lay on the pillow. With a contented sigh, she drifted back to sleep. I lay down too, trying to calm the heavy, painful beating of my heart. Exhausted but unable to rest, I stared at the ceiling, my mind racing. At breakfast, a voice in my head echoed, "Her last! her last!" and I felt relieved to see her eat. At lunch, even though she wasn't hungry, I insisted she eat while I abstained.

I informed my servant to take a few days off, explaining I would be out of town. Finally rid of him, I ordered a lavish dinner fit for a wedding feast, though I still couldn't touch a bite. Lucille ate, and it filled me with joy to see her happy. I can only imagine this is how a jailer feels when feasting a condemned prisoner before execution.

Later, I carefully laid out her new clothes on the bed, the finery that thrilled her so much. I laughed as I did it and then sat down to watch her get dressed. She was as delighted as a child, trying on each piece and admiring herself in the mirror with little exclamations of joy. I laced her suede shoes, helped fasten her dress, and buttoned her gloves. When she was ready, I wrapped her in a gray traveling cloak, hiding her pretty face under a thick veil.

I told her we would catch the midnight train to Buffalo, where we would get married and spend a few days at Niagara Falls before returning to New York. She trusted me completely and asked if she could add to her wardrobe before we returned. We planned to leave early enough to take a scenic drive before heading to the station.

Lucille had been cooped up in the house for so long that this plan felt like a breath of fresh air to her. She was buzzing with a mix of eagerness and nerves. I arranged for my horse and dog-cart to be ready at a precise hour. Late-night drives were a quirk of mine, so no one questioned my request. I stepped out of the house, instructing Lucille to make sure the door was locked and then walk to the corner of Fifth Avenue where I'd pick her up.

Just before we left, I invited Lucille to share a glass of wine with me. I discreetly added a sleeping potion to hers. As she raised her glass, she said, "Here's to our happiness."

I left my own glass untouched. Then she approached me with a tenderness I once found endearing. She lifted her veil and said, "Archie, kiss your little one."

I embraced her, my heart racing, breath heavy. Holding her close, I kissed her soft, warm lips with a touch of regret.

"Lucille," I said, my voice pleading, "can you go back to your home and forget about becoming my wife?"

"I'd rather die," she responded, her voice sharp with anger. It was clear then; there was no turning back. Either I needed to follow through with my plan or abandon all hopes of marrying Miss Chamberlain and accept Lucille as my wife.

"We've had such a wonderful two weeks, haven't we, Archie?" she said, her arms still around my neck. "Kiss your little one goodbye, for when I come back, I'll be your wife."

"Yes, when you come back," I murmured, kissing her again. In that fleeting moment, I imagined a serene home with her as my wife. Her beauty tugged at my heart, but the thought of giving up the wealth and status I yearned for snapped me back to reality. No, it was too late to indulge in such fantasies.

I reached the curb just as she got there, only stopping long enough for her to climb in. There was a valise in the dog-cart, which Lucille believed held a change of clothes.

I sped to the park, the tires humming on the asphalt. As we entered, Lucille let out a yawn and mentioned she was feeling sleepy. I kept my eyes sharp, scanning for any sign of movement or sounds that might reveal someone else's presence. As we reached a curve in the road and everything seemed calm, I asked Lucille to take the wheel for a moment, claiming I needed to check something on the car. She lazily agreed, taking hold of the steering wheel.

"Do you see anything ahead, Lucille?" I asked while reaching beneath the seat to pull out a sandbag I had stashed there earlier. Standing as if to step out and inspect the car, I gripped the sandbag tightly.

"No, Archie, the road looks clear," she said slowly, leaning forward for a better view. In that moment, I lifted the sandbag and brought it down on her head with swift precision. She made no sound, collapsing against the passenger door. I caught her with one hand and steadied the car with the other. I managed to pull her out and lay her gently on a nearby bench, her heartbeat already silent.

I removed her Connemara cloak and veil, taking a moment to arrange her into a seated position. Her hands clasped neatly in her lap, I struggled to balance her parasol on her knee, eventually letting it fall to the ground before her. I kissed her lips, still warm, and pulled her hat down to keep her eyes closed. Stashing the sandbag and her clothing into a valise, I drove back to the garage under cover of night.

Back at my apartment, I spent the rest of the night methodically burning her clothing. Just before dawn, I quietly slipped out and headed to the Gilsey House. There, I rented a room and collapsed into bed, finally letting sleep take me.

I woke up in the afternoon, and over breakfast, I read an early edition of the evening paper. It had a report about finding Lucille's body in Central Park. Enclosed in the smaller envelope is a photograph of Lucille before her hair was bleached; I'm sure you'll recognize her. I've also included the letter she wrote to her mother. Now you understand why Maggie Williams' tears unnerved me so much and why I was horrified when I saw the man suspected of my crime at the Hoffman House. My overwhelming guilt kept me from telling you my name, and when you came to my apartment looking for Lucille, I knew my time was up.

I could have fought and delayed the inevitable, but what would have been the point? Even if the evidence wasn't enough to hang me, it was certainly enough to imprison me—the waiters, my servant, and the cab driver all would have testified against me, building a solid case of circumstantial evidence. I choose death instead.

It's morning now—the morning of the day that was supposed to be my wedding day. Oh God, I had a wild hope when I started writing this confession, but it's gone now. This is the end. If there's any compassion within you, please show me some mercy.

Archie Stammen

North Washington Square, June 7, 18—

CHAPTER SEVENTEEN

S teve could barely get dressed fast enough after reading Archie Stammen's letter. Usually laid-back, he was now caught in a frenzy of urgency. The elevator felt agonizingly slow. Bursting out onto the street, he hopped into the first cab he saw, urging the driver to speed to Fifth Avenue.

In her cozy little room, Stephanie Orton was nervously awaiting her dashing lover. Her face was marked with sorrow and regret, her apologies rehearsed and ready. But Steve gave her no chance to utter them.

"Stephanie, I've cracked the mystery!" he shouted, and pulling her into a tight embrace, he held her so close she nearly lost her breath.

"I've got the whole story, sweetheart," he said, and with brief, urgent words, interspersed with Stephanie's gasps of shock and sorrow, Steve recounted all that had happened since the night she left for Washington.

"My dear, oh, Steve. Good morning," Stephanie's aunt interrupted as she entered the room, still in her house dress but hastily wrapped in a carriage cloak. "Mrs. Chamberlain just sent for me. They've received news that Clara's fiancé, Mr. Stammen, was found dead in his bathroom, a gunshot wound to the head. They believe it was an accident. Poor Clara, who was supposed to be a bride tonight, is completely devastated. I'll return soon. Steve, stay with her."

They let the aunt leave without revealing what they knew, and, oblivious to the outside world, they read Archie Stammen's confession. Tears streamed down Stephanie's face, her heart aching as much for the troubled man as for the devastated Clara.

"I knew he was involved," Steve said. "When the messenger boy identified the man at the Hoffman House as resembling the one who bought the gown, it clicked for me—though this man was fair-haired and Archie Stammen was dark. As soon as I noticed the resemblance, the whole scenario fell into place in my mind. My offhand joke about the man being bleached planted the idea that maybe Maggie's sister had bleached her hair after she left home."

Still, it was all so wild and improbable that I tried not to dwell on it.

Determined to shield Archie Stammen's name from further disgrace, even if he hardly deserved it, they agreed to share the secret of the crime only with those directly involved. Mrs. Van Brunt returned from the house where the wedding preparations had been abruptly transformed into arrangements for a funeral. Stephanie, eyes red from crying, pulled her aunt into her small study where Steve was waiting. Together, they recounted the astonishing tale to the already grief-stricken woman. She was even more resolved than they were to keep the confession confidential. Making it public would help no one and would only bring more pain to the family who had expected to welcome Archie as their future son- in-law.

They had planned to visit Maggie Williams that day to tell her about her sister's tragic fate. However, Mrs. Van Brunt, always the more considerate one, advised them to delay delivering the sad news until after Maggie's upcoming marriage on Sunday, as Steve had mentioned. Archie Stammen was quietly buried that Sunday, departing from the Chamberlain mansion, while his would-be bride lay unconscious in a darkened room upstairs. As an old and close friend of Mrs. Chamberlain, Mrs. Van Brunt attended the funeral, and Stephanie accompanied her, her heart torn between compassion for the dead man, the murdered girl, and the grieving Chamberlain daughter.

If Archie Stammen had survived, Stephanie would have loathed him for his terrible crime. Yet, given his decision to end his own life, she couldn't help but pity his miserable end. That Sunday evening, they visited Maggie Williams, now Mrs. Martin Shanks, where Stephanie delicately shared the story of the Central Park Mystery, carefully leaving out the more painful details about her sister's involvement. Rough but tender-hearted, Martin Shanks did his best to comfort his new bride.

Kelly Morgan's tears mingled with Maggie's, but an unspoken tension hung in the air. She struggled to find her voice in the presence of Stephanie Orton, despite Stephanie's best efforts to be friendly and considerate. The warm, easy rapport that once existed between Kelly and Steve had vanished. Steve tried to maintain a facade of friendliness, but Kelly's icy silence left him feeling an odd sense of relief when he and Stephanie finally departed.

"Stephanie, Archie Stammen was right: happiness isn't something we can afford to let slip away when it's within reach," Steve said, his voice tinged with melancholy as he and Stephanie drove homeward. Stephanie responded only with a sigh.

"I didn't solve the mystery the way you hoped," he continued, grasping her hand gently, "but I refuse to be cheated out of my happiness. When will you marry me?"

Stephanie tried to feign surprise, but her trembling hand betrayed her. "Oh!"

"This is the tenth," Steve said, a mix of authority and tenderness in his voice. "I'll give you until the twenty-first to make whatever preparations you need for the wedding."

Stephanie sighed, half in exasperation, half in contentment. "If you put it that way, I suppose I must meekly obey," she said, yielding as she let Steve envelop her in his arms.

The End.

Made in United States
Troutdale, OR
12/08/2024

26112002R00066